THE GHOST OF THE
PHOENIX

To Thelma,
For your thoughtful editing
that made this book so much
better. Thank you and happy
reading!
S.Grant

S. G. GRANT

authorHOUSE®

AuthorHouse™
1663 Liberty Drive
Bloomington, IN 47403
www.authorhouse.com
Phone: 1-800-839-8640

First published by AuthorHouse   10/17/2011

ISBN: 978-1-4670-0790-0 (sc)

Printed in the United States of America

Any people depicted in stock imagery provided by Thinkstock are models, and such images are being used for illustrative purposes only.
Certain stock imagery © Thinkstock.

This book is printed on acid-free paper.

For my brothers, though we may have gone our separate ways I hope this is one journey we can share together.

PROLOGUE

Seven prophecies are set to be completed,
an ancient ritual by seven monks will be repeated
Through seven worlds of the dead, there shall rise,
seven shadows returning from the skies
On the seven paths carved of stone,
the seven phoenixes will reclaim their throne
Now seven stones that once were lost, reunite,
granted immortality, evil will rise to the highest height
Eternity of air, earth, fire, ice, lava, water and death,
after the final battle only one will take breath
Heroes born to the sons of those betrayed, seeking a
diary on a body decayed
Encased in this poem for children,
the location for final hope is hidden
Nowhere to run, nowhere to hide,
a third will have to choose their side

Guided by the hand of fate,
raised to see the world they helped create
Every path leads to a single place,
and on the longest day, good and evil meet face to face

CHAPTER ONE
SHADOWS IN THE NIGHT

High in the sky the silvery crescent of the moon was peering through a thin layer of cloud. Its light filtering down through the last remaining leaves on the forest of beech trees. On the edge of a small clearing a deer shifted tentatively, careful not to disturb the golden brown foliage of the ferns.

Out of the darkness a fiery oval erupted into existence. For several minutes it hung there, the flames that surrounded the edges lapping lazily in the cold night air. Watching on, the deer stood captivated by the circling flames.

A crack resonated around the hollow as a hooded figure appeared, stumbling from the shimmering oval. Moments later another followed and then a third.

Straightening up the figure gripped his wooden staff for support, freezing when he noticed the deer in the shadows. Slowly he raised a hand, brushing the hood back.

In an instant the deer turned, fleeing into the darkness that was held amongst the trees. Quietly he laughed, the empty, wretched sound breaking the silence. Slowly he pulled the hood back over his head, turning to face the other two that stood close by.

In the light of the portal their shadows stretched over the barren ground. Raising a hand, he gestured in the direction of the portal. With a crack and a flurry of fiery sparks it disappeared. The only sign of its existence, a scorch mark in the dusty soil.

"Come," he breathed. Without hesitation the other two, who had so far remained silent, followed him towards the dark trees.

"Where are we?" whispered one of the followers, her voice inquisitive and yet demanding. For several long minutes the leading figure remained silent, appearing not to have heard her.

As they stepped out from between the trees her question was answered. On the slight downward incline sat a jumble of small houses, each of them looking identical at a distance. On the far side of the village a church spire climbed towards the sky. All of the buildings were dark except for one, sitting half a mile or so from where they stood.

"Welcome to the tiny settlement of Gladstow," said the man. Lifting his staff he gestured in the direction of the only light in the village. "That is our target for tonight. Inside we will find a man, William, he will be of great help to us."

Silently, the three cloaked figures moved along the cobbled streets between the tiny houses. It was not long before they stood outside the small building he had indicated earlier from their vantage point. Lifting his staff he used it to knock on the wooden door. Somewhere inside there was the sound of tired movement. Moments later the door creaked open an inch. In the gap a brown eye appeared, shielded behind a pair of square wire frame glasses.

"C-can I-I help y-you?" stuttered the man as he looked at the cloaked figures.

"You are William?" rasped the cloaked man, moving forwards into the light that flooded from inside the house.

"Y-yes," he replied as he looked under the hood. "N-no, it's y-you." Crying out, he slammed the door shut and the sound of his hurried footsteps could be heard from outside.

Anger began to rise within the cloaked man as he raised the staff, a jet of white light blasting the door inwards. It would have been just as easy to open the door with his hand but he felt the way he had chosen to be more intimidating. Stepping over the threshold his eyes, hidden in the shadow of the hood, searched for the man.

From somewhere out of sight he heard a soft whimper. Slowly turning on the spot he looked in the direction of a wooden workbench that had been pushed away from the wall. With a sigh he raised the staff again, an identical jet of white light erupting from it, this time launching the workbench aside. With a resounding crash it hit the wall opposite, splintering into dozens of pieces.

Cowering in a tight ball sat the man, now exposed in his hiding place. Covering the space between them in several long strides the cloaked man grabbed him by the neck of his baggy white shirt. Without a care for his surroundings he extinguished the candles with a wave of his hand and began to drag the shaking wreck of a man towards the door.

The second he stepped outside he became aware that the noise from the house had alerted the villagers. Some of them stood in their doorways, peering into the murky darkness while others were huddled in groups whispering urgently. Trying to blend in with the darkness he looked around for his followers.

A blinding flash of red streaked out from behind two of the buildings, striking one of the men in a small gathering in the chest. Instantly he was blasted back, crashing against the wall of the house with a sickening crunch. Pandemonium and panic spread through the villagers like wildfire as they all dived for cover.

Beneath his hood a thin smile twitched across his lips as he saw the two followers striding out of the darkness, staffs raised. Through the chaos that reigned in the narrow street he dragged his captive unnoticed towards the edge of the forest.

Less than half an hour later he stood on the hillside looking down on the small town, his two followers standing silent behind him. Between the pair of them they held the struggling man tightly.

The moon had now disappeared behind a blanket of cloud that glowed orange from the fires in the village. As the three left they set alight several small buildings on the outskirts of the village. Even at their distance he could hear the screams of the women and children as they tried to put out the fires in the nearby crop fields with the little water they had.

Laughing his eerily hollow laugh again he raised his staff one last time, directing it to the sky above. For a second it appeared that nothing had happened, that was until the clouds began to swirl, spiralling faster and faster. With a thunderous crack a bolt of lightning flashed through the sky, striking somewhere in the centre of the village.

Behind him he heard the sound of their captive screaming as William tried to escape again. The air filled with a high pitched cackling laugh from the cloaked woman behind him as she applauded enthusiastically.

"Stop," he commanded her before turning to William who now hung helplessly in the arms of his other follower before him.

"What do you want from me?" he spat, not daring to look under the hood of the man who stood facing him.

"The legend of the stones," he whispered. "Tell me everything you know about it."

"I don't know what you're talking about," William replied weakly.

"Lies," the hooded man bellowed.

"I'll die before I say a word," he said defiantly, summoning all the strength he could to stand before the cloaked man.

"Really?" he asked, raising his staff slightly. When William didn't answer he made a sharp jabbing movement with the staff that left William screaming every obscenity that came to his mind.

"N-never," he stuttered as his tortured mind begged him to give up the information he had spent the last thirty three years of his life gathering.

"You will tell me everything you know. Even if I have to drag you back to that town and make you watch as I kill each and every one of them before your eyes," he whispered menacingly as he reached for the hood that covered his head for the second time that night.

"N-no, p-please," he begged. "P-please, I'll t-tell you e-everything."

Hatred welled up inside him as he stared down at the pathetic, and now sobbing, man before him. Raising his staff again he allowed his anger to flow through it, tormenting the mind of his prisoner again.

"The stones, where are they?" he demanded as he released the curse on William.

"T-the legend says that they are scattered across the world, h-hidden in the caves of their g-guardians," William replied quietly, his voice hollow with the betrayal he was committing.

"You know where they are hidden?" he asked, pleased that his torture had finally yielded some results.

"N-no, if I knew I would have tried to take them," he replied. As he saw the staff being raised again he hurried to continue before his torture resumed. "T-there is a b-book. T-the diary of an explorer, it is s-supposed to contain the l-locations of the s-stones."

"Where is the book?"

"Lost. The explorer took it with him when he went searching for one of the stones. He never returned," William muttered, his head bowing slightly as he silently apologised for all the damage he was about to do. "When the stones are united they are said to make the holder immortal."

Somewhere under the dark hood William saw the thin lips curve into a sickening smile. As he saw the staff raised again he braced himself for more pain. But none came. Instead they were cast into the light of a fiery portal that had erupted out of thin air.

"See, that wasn't so hard, now, was it?" the cloaked man hissed with a laugh. "I have further need for you. You will accompany me until I am done with you. If you do your job well I may just let you return to this pathetic village, not that there will be much left," he said with a glance over at the burning fields and buildings.

In the light cast by the flickering flames he could make out the silhouettes of the villagers still hurrying to extinguish the fires. With a loud merciless laugh that was left echoing across the landscape he stepped into the portal, pushing William ahead of him. A split second later it was wiped from existence again, leaving nothing but a scorch mark behind.

CHAPTER TWO

THE DARK MOVEMENT

In a flurry of green sparks a teenage boy appeared. Just shy of his eighteenth birthday he stood at almost six foot, his straight brown hair hung down across his eyes, thrown out of place by his journey.

Raising a tanned arm he brushed it aside with his fingers to reveal soft brown eyes hiding behind it. Shaking his head slightly he adjusted to his new surroundings. From the moment he had arrived he could sense that there was something different. There was a spark in the air, unlike the one that would linger after a storm.

Bending down he took his bag by the strap, feeling the soft sheepskin slide over his fingers. Quickly throwing it over one shoulder he started the short walk down to the village, eager to see everyone again.

As he drew closer the sensation he had felt when he had first arrived was confirmed. Something was different.

Several of the small houses on the nearest side of the village were blackened and burnt. There was no one wandering the streets, no one out working the land.

Quickening his pace as much as he could in his stiff, creaseless black trousers he entered the village. As he passed the burnt out houses he saw that the damage was far worse than he had made out on the hillside. There was a slight twinge of sadness as he passed the destroyed home of Sally Walker, the kind, elderly lady who had often looked after him when he was younger.

Everyone in Gladstow was part of the close-knit community. It was their way of life, the way they survived. On a normal day there would be people outside throwing him a 'Welcome back' or a 'Good to see you again' as he returned from one of his trips to the city. Without constantly stopping to greet people it was five minutes later that he found himself outside the small single storey house belonging to his parents.

Reaching out he knocked on the slightly warped wooden door. It was only a matter of moments before the door flew open and his mother threw herself at him, holding on for dear life. After staggering back slightly with the enthusiastic welcome he managed to prise her off him.

It was from her that he had inherited his soft brown eyes and straight brown hair, although he preferred to keep his far shorter. Ushering him towards the lone chair beside the fire she took his bag, placing it in the corner by the door.

"Tell me all about it," she said, handing him a cup of dark red liquid as he took his seat on the rickety wooden chair while she resumed her preparations for the evening meal. For a minute he stayed silent, taking a long drink from the cup. It was raspberry juice from this year's harvest, heated up on the fire just the way he liked it.

"It was great," he replied as he looked at the plain oak panel walls fondly, remembering all the details of the panels and the metal candle holders that held the light source of the room. "Although it looks like I missed something here while I was gone. What happened?"

"You saw the burnt out houses on your way into the village?" she questioned without looking up from the small fire she was tending. "Must have been about a week ago it happened now."

"What happened?" he repeated.

"It was terrible. We were asleep when it happened. There was this tremendous bang from somewhere outside. When your father went to check it out he said there were people outside. Out of nowhere there was this streak of red light and it hit poor old Oliver who works the corn fields. He's fine," she added hastily as a look of concern crossed his face. "There were these people, three of them. They were all huddled up in these long cloaks with hoods over their heads. It wasn't until the next morning we realised they had taken him."

"Who did they take?"

"They took William," she replied.

"Why did they take him?" he asked. William was an elderly man known throughout the village for the amount of time he spent with his research and his books.

"I don't know," she said quietly. "They must think he knows something that will help them."

"Does anyone know who took him?" he asked, his curiosity getting the better of him.

"There was a rumour going around that it was The Dark Movement," she said. "No one was really sure though, it all happened at night."

"What would The Dark Movement want with Gladstow though?"

"No idea." She mused as she gave the fire a small prod with another piece of wood. "Tell me about what you did in the city. It's been almost a month since you were last here Nicolas."

"For once can't you just call me Nick, everyone else does," he said, rolling his eyes at his mother.

"You were born as Nicolas. I will not call you by any other name," she said sternly.

"Fine," Nick muttered under his breath. "The usual really, a bit of work now and then, other than that I spent a lot of the time studying in the library."

"Did you meet anyone nice while you were there?" she asked, returning to her usual kind tone.

"No," he replied, knowing that his mother was about to begin her lecture of finding a partner.

"I'm sure if you just tried to-" she started, stopping mid sentence when Nick set his cup down and stood up.

"I haven't even been back an hour and you are already trying to find me a wife. Why can't you just leave it?" Nick asked, moving towards the door. "I'm going to see who else I can find around the village."

Leaving his mother to prepare the evening meal he wandered towards the village square. Since he had arrived back he hadn't seen anyone out in the village, it seemed completely lifeless. That was when his eye caught on William's house, the door hanging crookedly from its frame. Pausing for a moment to stick his head inside he decided to head out to the crop fields.

Sure enough when he arrived he found some of the villagers working in the fields. Over by one of the old raspberry canes he saw his father picking the few that remained. Smiling to himself he headed in that direction, waving to Oliver in the next field as he passed, pleased to see that he really was alright.

"Hey," Nick called when he got within earshot of his father. Watching he saw his father straighten up behind the canes he was currently picking from, a smile breaking across his lips when he saw Nick walking towards him.

"Nick, you're back," his father called as he leant on the old wooden post that held the canes up, brushing his long thinning grey hair away from his light blue eyes. The only time he ever consented to shorten Nick's name was when his wife wasn't around. "I thought you weren't gettin' back 'til later."

"I decided to leave a bit earlier," Nick replied. "Looks like I missed quite a lot while I was gone."

"Has your mother already told you about what happened last week?" he asked.

"Bits and pieces, she just said some cloaked figures from The Dark Movement turned up and took William," Nick said.

"They burnt down some houses and set a couple of fields on fire but that sounds like she told you everythin' else," he replied as he picked up the wicker basket of raspberries from the ground and rested it on the post.

"You think it was The Dark Movement?" Nick asked, reaching out to take one of the raspberries.

"Could've been," his father replied after a moment. "Thomas from the house next to William's swears one of the people was Numquam himself."

"What do you think?" Nick said as he made to take another of the raspberries.

"Hey! Don't eat 'em all," his father said as he pulled the basket away from Nick. "I'm not so sure. It's not like him to get involved in somethin' like this."

"Sorry," Nick said apologetically as he threw the berry back in the basket.

"It's nothin'. You should go find that girl; she's been looking for you since you left. Much to your mother's displeasure I might add," he said with a laugh.

"Rose?" Nick asked questioningly. "Did she say what she wanted?"

"That's the one," he replied tapping his fingers on the wicker basket. "Just wanted to see you I think."

Bidding farewell to his father, Nick turned his mind to any place where Rose could be. Knowing her she would be outside somewhere having argued with her mother again. Even though her temper could flare in an instant she usually spent her time somewhere quiet, more often than not with a book in front of her.

Turning his mind back towards the events that had taken place in the village while he was away, he allowed his legs to carry him down the slope towards the lake.

Approaching the lake he saw the water shimmering in the late afternoon sunlight. By the water's edge a clump of willow trees was growing, their branches hanging low, swaying lazily in the slight breeze that had picked up. Taking in the scene before him it was a moment before he spotted the sun reflecting off something by one of the trees.

Sitting at the base of one of the willow trees was Rose, her midnight black hair reflecting the sunlight. As he had expected she was resting a book in her lap, oblivious to the stunning sunset that was starting to form over the lake in front of her.

"Hey bookworm," he called out to her. There was a flash as the light reflecting off her hair passed his face. In seconds she was on her feet and running up the slight slope towards him, her book lying forgotten in the grass. Taking note that her white dress seemed to have been torn off around knee height, probably by Rose herself, was all he could do before everything around him disappeared into her black hair as she threw her arms around him, knocking him back slightly.

"Too tight," he managed to breathe as she squeezed him as if she hadn't seen him in years. After a moment he felt her grip relax slightly.

"Sorry," she whispered sheepishly in reply. "I missed you."

"I figured as much," he said with a laugh as he gently eased her off him. Stepping back slightly she looked up at him. Normally she was only two or three inches shorter than him but the slope wasn't helping.

"I missed you loads," she repeated quietly.

"Apparently you were looking for me every day since I left," Nick said, nudging her back in the direction of the lake.

"Says who?" she asked after a minute. Picking up her book he sat down on the grassy bank before he decided to reply.

"My father," he said grinning at her. After a moment her smile faded.

"Your mother doesn't seem too happy about it though," she said quietly. "Did she . . ."

"You know what my mother is like," Nick replied. "She has something against nearly everyone."

"Did you miss me?" Rose asked suddenly. Caught slightly off guard by her question Nick hesitated.

"Of course I did," he replied, glancing across at her, he saw her pale blue eyes staring back at him. She had sat down beside him at some point and was leaning half against the willow tree and half against him, neither of them particularly interested in the sunset that had cast the crystal clear water of the lake a vivid orange. "Tell me about what happened while I was gone."

"Other than that night about a week ago, nothing interesting," she sighed as she leant her head on his shoulder. Gently he slid her sideways so she was leaning against the tree again. "Sorry."

"It's nothing," Nick replied. "What were you reading?"

"Just some ridiculous tale about some stones that make people immortal," she whispered. "William lent it to me before he disappeared.

"Did you see the door to his house?" Nick asked, only realising what a stupid question it was after he had said it, of course she would have seen it.

"I only glanced inside but it looked like a real mess in there," she said. "I guess I should put that book back, I finished it just before you got here."

"What were you doing when I got here, it looked like you were reading," Nick said.

"Just thinking."

"What about?" he asked, nudging her in the side gently. "You know how bad I am when it comes to guessing."

"It's your birthday in three days," she said quietly. "What do you want?"

"Nothing really," he considered. "What do you want? It's yours in a couple of months as well."

When she stayed silent he looked up at her. Quickly she brushed aside a stray hair that was blowing over her eyes. Looking away he let his fingers pick at the soft grass beside him. Over the lake the sun was beginning to set, turning the sky a deep red.

"We should get back," he said suddenly as he pushed himself back to his feet. Slowly he turned and began to walk away. Somewhere behind him he heard the sound of Rose following after him.

"Nick, wait," she called after him. Stopping in his tracks he waited for her to catch up with him. "I'm going to put the book back tonight, after dark."

"Why are you telling me this?" he asked, confused by what had brought the topic of the book up again.

"I want you to come with me," she replied instantly. "You said you wanted to know what happened last week as well."

"Fine," he sighed after a minute of silence.

"Meet me by the stone in the village square after dark," she whispered as they passed one of the villagers. With a wave and a radiant smile she turned and jogged around the corner between two of the houses, disappearing in the direction of her own.

For several minutes he stood completely still, thinking about everything that had happened since he had returned from the city. All the mystery that The Dark Movement had left behind, and yet nothing could shake from his mind the image of her blue eyes staring back at him. Putting it to one side for now, he turned and headed home.

It was just after darkness had fallen in Gladstow when Nick eased open the door and slipped outside. With a small candle lantern in one hand he crept between the houses, heading for the centre of the village. With no sign of anyone around he made quick progress.

When he entered the small village square, that bore no resemblance whatsoever to a square, he noticed a faint candlelight in the centre. Cautiously he approached, careful not to make any noise. Relaxing he realised that it was only Rose. She was sitting beside the centre stone, her knees drawn up to her chest, her head buried in her arms. Surrounding her were pieces of rock that looked to have been blasted away from the central stone.

"Rose," he whispered gently. When she didn't respond he reached out and put a hand on her shoulder. In an instant her head snapped up, looking him straight in the eye. "What's wrong?"

"My mother threw me out. Again," she said bitterly as she rested her chin on her arms.

"What happened?" Nick asked quietly.

"Something about wasting my time with stupid b-books, being rebellious, the usual," she replied in a choked whisper as a tear trickled down her cheek. Gently he reached out and pulled her closer to him. Rose had always been having arguments with her mother for as long as he could remember, more so since her father had disappeared.

For ten minutes they sat in the village square, the only source of light was their two candle lanterns as Rose cried on Nick's shoulder.

"Come on, we need to take your book back," Nick said quietly as he stood up. Slowly she nodded before accepting his hand and allowing him to pull her up.

"Thanks," she whispered as they headed towards William's house.

"Thanks for what?" Nick asked, slightly confused by what she was referring to. Glancing down he saw that she was still clinging to his hand as if it were her only lifeline.

"Coming to take my book back with me," she said. "After getting thrown out by my mother I don't want you getting in trouble as well."

"It's alright. What are you going to do tonight?" he asked as they turned the corner. Ahead of them stood William's house, the door still hanging half open from the attack a week ago.

"I don't know," she confessed, glancing across at him in the hope that he might know what to do. When he didn't reply she looked away again, dropping his hand.

Together they stepped through the broken doorway and into the house. The room they found themselves in was cluttered; a shattered workbench lay in pieces around the room. Slowly Rose picked her way through the debris towards the large bookshelf at the far end of the room.

In the half-light cast by the candle he looked around him, his eyes lingering on Rose's hair that appeared to shimmer in the dark. Looking down he saw a small rug that had obviously been disturbed by someone recently. Under the corner that had been moved he could make out what looked like a crack in the floor boards.

"Hey, come take a look at this," Nick whispered, looking up to where Rose was still looking at the bookshelf. As she turned he saw her wipe a tear away from her cheek as she looked at the place he was gesturing to. "What do you think? Could it be a trapdoor?"

"Does it matter?" she asked, impatient and eager to get out of the house as quickly as possible.

"Maybe it has something to do with why they came here," Nick said, his curiosity edging into his voice.

"Well there's only one way to find out," she whispered as she pulled at the edge of the board. The rug fell back as the board lifted, revealing darkness beneath. When he looked up at her there was a twinkle in her sapphire eyes that he hadn't seen since they had been by the lake. With a nod to her, he stepped into the unknown.

Chapter Three

THE IMMORTALITY STONES

As he climbed down the small wooden ladder Nick realised that the candle in his lantern was beginning to get close to burning out. Somewhere above him he could hear Rose moving around. Holding up the lantern he looked around him. The walls were rough, lines of rocks holding out the soil that pressed against the basement.

"What is this place?" Rose asked as she dropped lightly to the floor beside him.

"No idea," Nick replied a moment later. "You want to go back?"

"No point really, it's not like I can go back home," she whispered, trying desperately to hide her emotion in the dark. Throwing her a reassuring smile, Nick began to move deeper into the basement. With the little light that they had from their lanterns they found a small tunnel entrance in one of the rock faces. With a confirming nod to each other, they continued deeper in to the cavern.

Along the rocky walls of the tunnel stubby remains of candles that had long since burnt out hung in their elegant holders. Yet why go to the trouble when no one was meant to see them? Did this place hold a purpose when William was younger? What did it mean now?

Pausing at one of the candle holders, Nick raised his lantern for a closer look. The metal was twisted and warped, forming the shape of an ivy leaf and a runner that curled around the base of the candle.

"It looks like the leaf on the cover of that book he let me borrow," Rose whispered. The silence that filled the air was broken by the sound of dripping water somewhere up ahead. Acknowledging what she had said with a nod he turned away from the ornate candle holder, quietly moving towards the sound of water, Rose trailing behind him.

Stepping out of the tunnel they found themselves staring into darkness. Cautiously taking a step forward, Nick felt the ground beneath his foot sink slightly. Behind him Nick heard a gasp from Rose as the candles around the room flared into life, burning as if they had never been extinguished.

Blinking, Nick waited for his eyes to adjust. In the centre of the room, jagged white rock made up the pillar that supported the ceiling above them. Behind him he could hear a soft scraping as Rose shuffled her feet.

"What is this place?" she asked, watching as Nick's eyebrows crinkled slightly before he answered.

"I have no idea," he replied truthfully, moving further into the room. "The pillar in the centre, is it me or does it look like the stone in the centre of the village?"

"A little bit," Rose said, ignoring the smile that played across Nick's lips as she tilted her head to one side for another angle. The smile was wiped off his face moments later when Rose nudged him in the side as she walked past him.

"What was that for?" Nick asked, feigning pain as he turned to see where she was going. She didn't reply, just glanced back and flashed a glittering smile at him. For several minutes they remained silent, Nick watching as Rose looked closely at the stone.

"It's the same type of stone," she said as she peered round the side to look at Nick. "Whereabouts under the village do you think we are?"

"You think it could be the same stone, don't you?"

"It's the same type of rock, although I have no idea how it got to be so battered," she said, running the tips of her fingers along one of the scratches.

Out of the corner of his eye Nick saw something sparkle for a split second in the candle light. Crinkling an eyebrow, he placed his lantern down and moved over to investigate.

In the shadowy corner of the underground room a wooden rack stood beside the wall. At one side of the rack a sword was held in place, its blade perfectly sharpened to a point. Crouching down he grasped the handle, lifting it. Laying the blade across his palm he looked down at the hilt. Beneath the decorative pattern a pure black stone was embedded. Two words were engraved in to the metal: Nex Vesica.

"Rose," Nick called out, looking around to see where she had gone. When she didn't respond he stood up. With the sword still in his hand he moved back out into the centre of the room. "Rose?"

Somewhere to his left he heard movement and instinctively lifted the sword into a defensive position as he turned. Standing in the mouth of another tunnel was Rose, her eyes unfocussed as she looked at him. Lowering the sword again he grasped the blade, holding out the hilt for her to look at.

"Do you know what 'Nex Vesica' means?" Nick asked when her eyes flicked to the sword.

"Where did you find that?" Rose demanded, her voice rising above her normal tone.

"Over there," Nick replied uncertainly, vaguely gesturing over his shoulder. Without warning she grabbed the hilt and pulled it out of his hands. Feeling the sting of the blade he jumped back, his eyes staring wildly at her sudden change of mood. Turning over his hands he saw blood seeping from a cut that ran across his palm. "What is wrong with you?"

Ignoring him, Rose just stared back at him, her blue eyes burning in a way he had never seen. Slowly her eyes began to drop towards the sword again, freezing when she saw the blood on Nick's right hand. With a gasp she dropped the sword with a clang as if it had burnt her. Slowly her eyes began to return to their normal, light shade of blue.

"W-what happened?" Rose stuttered, her eyes not leaving the cut.

"What are you on about?" Nick spat venomously. "You just pulled that sword out of my hands."

"I-I did?" Rose questioned, watching as the look of anger on Nick's face turned to concern.

"I asked you what 'Nex Vesica' meant. When you looked down at the sword you pulled it out of my hands," Nick replied, watching her face for any sign of recognition.

"Sorry," Rose muttered, looking down at her feet. "I don't know what happened. The last thing I remember was walking in to the tunnel and then I was here, looking at the cut on your hand." Seeing how shaken she was by it he decided to drop it.

"Do you know what 'Nex Vesica' means?" he asked quietly.

"I'm not sure about 'Nex'," she said after a moment. "Vesica is Latin for blade though."

"It's a start I suppose, we can look it up later," Nick said as he watched her run a hand through her long black hair.

"Sorry," Rose replied meekly.

Taking the sword in his left hand Nick returned it to the small rack. All the while Rose, staying by the tunnel, stared blankly at something only she could see. As the flow of blood from his palm began to stop he walked back to her, watching her closely as he approached.

"Are you alright," he whispered as he reached out with his clean hand and rested it on her shoulder. Nodding slowly she looked at him for a moment. Burying her face in his shoulder she began to apologise again.

For several long minutes that could have stretched into hours they stood in silence. Slowly she began to relax as she tried to forget what had happened.

"We should get out of here," Nick said quietly in her ear. Slowly he eased her off him so that she stood in front of him again.

"No," she replied, her determination seeping into her voice. "I need to know what happened to me." Reluctantly he agreed. As much as he hated it, he knew she always had a way of getting what she wanted.

"I'll go see what is down here," Nick said, gesturing to the tunnel." You should stay here." As he finished he saw her look up, her eyes telling him to give up and that she was coming with him. Sighing in exasperation he turned to face the tunnel.

For the first few seconds after he entered the tunnel everything felt normal. Then the temperature dropped drastically, as if he had just walked into an ice storm.

"What was that?" Rose asked from behind him as she passed through the barrier.

"Not sure," Nick replied as he glanced back at her. "How are you feeling?"

"A little cold," Rose said. "I'm fine," she added when she saw him look at her questioningly. Nodding acceptingly he fell silent. He knew she wasn't feeling fine but the willingness to avoid an argument overwhelmed him.

In his concern he hadn't noticed the candle flames change colour. The burning orange had been replaced by an icy cold blue flame. From somewhere deeper in the tunnels there was a faint humming sound, combined with that of dripping water.

Slowly the tunnel began to widen, more flickering blue light flowing in from the room at the end. At the entrance to the room the air seemed to shimmer and ripple. Cautiously Nick and Rose approached, stopping just short. The room on the other side was blurred and distorted. Listening closely the sound of the dripping water was coming from the barrier before them.

Glancing at each other they saw their own confusion reflected in the face of the other. Slowly Nick reached out until the tip of his finger was as close to the barrier as it could be without touching it.

"What do you think it is?" Rose asked warily as she watched Nick reaching out.

"I guess there's only one way to find out," he replied. Taking a breath he moved his finger closer until it touched the surface of the barrier. It was the strangest sensation he had ever felt. As the water broke around his finger the skin began to prickle. Somewhere at the tip of his finger he could feel warmth from the other side.

Removing his finger he found it to still be as dry as it had been before he had put it through the barrier. Turning, he saw Rose looking at him questioningly.

"I think it's safe to go through it," he whispered. Taking her hand in his own blood free one, he moved towards the shimmering surface.

As he passed through the water his skin prickled, a wave flowed through him. He felt safe. Secure. Moments later Rose appeared beside him, the same perplexed look etched on her face.

Looking at him she saw that he was looking over her shoulder. Turning, she found herself face to face with a barrier of flames. Quickly she jumped back, watching as the tallest licked at the ceiling of the tunnel like a fiery tongue.

The sound of something humming caused Nick to turn away from the flames. In the centre of the room was a white stone pillar, identical to the one they had seen before. Too identical, Nick decided as he moved closer to it.

"This is the same room," Nick whispered as he felt Rose brush past him, her hand leaving his.

"How can it be? We didn't turn any corners," Rose said, moving round the central column.

"Look, there's the rack with the sword on it," he said, pointing to the far corner where the metal was glinting in the candle light.

"Then why is this book case here?" Rose asked from somewhere out of sight.

"There wasn't a . . ." Nick muttered, breaking off when he moved around the column and saw it beside Rose. With a smirk she turned away from him, her attention focused on the books.

Shaking his head in disbelief, Nick looked around the room, spotting a battered wooden desk that had been pushed up against one of the rough walls.

Drawing closer, the faint humming he had heard in the tunnels seemed to grow louder. In the centre of the desk sat a circular slab of white rock. Seven rounded dips had been carved into the stone, five of which held large stones. Each of the stones held a different colour, forming a rainbow around the central hole. Around the edge of the tablet two words had been etched in the stone, over and over again, forming a continuous circle.

Peering closer Nick noticed more words, their tiny letters looping around each of the holes. The humming seemed to be coming from inside the stones themselves and as he looked closer they seemed to vibrate slightly.

"Rose! Come take a look at this," he called to her as he looked down at the stones. Behind him he heard the sound of her footsteps drawing closer. Recognising the words as Latin he turned to look at her. "Can you translate this?"

For a minute she stood in silence, bent over as she read the tablet. Nick watched on as a perplexed look flashed across her face.

"Immortalis Calx," she said, gesturing to the words around the edge. "This says Immortality Stones. The others all seem to be elemental. Fire, water, air, earth, ice and lava." Rose continued, pointing to each of the stones as she listed each of the words.

"What about the middle one? Nex?" Nick asked, indicating the empty central hole. Apart from the one she had named as lava, it was the only one that remained empty.

"I'm not sure. That was inscribed on the sword as well."

With a sigh Nick mustered a smile which Rose happily returned. There was something captivating about the stones.

"Can you hear them humming?" he asked quietly, trying not to talk over the sound.

"No," Rose replied bluntly, shaking her head she moved back towards the bookcase.

Somewhere inside, he sensed that she was still dwelling on the incident that had happened with the sword. Finding one of the words that had been on the hilt again had brought those thoughts back to her mind, although she tried not to show it. He knew that he should go and check on her but the stones had some kind of gravitational pull on him, holding him next to them.

Subconsciously he reached out a hand. As his fingers grasped the pale blue stone that represented ice a shock flew through his arm. In the split second that it took for him to register the pain there was a flash of blue light and an echoing bang. Everything around him went dark as he felt his feet leave the ground.

Out of the blackness a blue light came into view, growing larger with each passing second. Wherever he was, there was no sense of movement or direction. All he could do was watch and wait as the light grew closer. It was a bird of some kind

Gently it flapped its large wings as it stopped before him, slowly tilting its head, taking in Nick as he stood before it.

"What are you?" Nick asked more of himself than the creature before him, not expecting to receive an answer.

"I am the guardian of the ice stone," a low voice replied from the darkness. The bird didn't move a muscle. "Years ago the stone was removed from its home by a man. Mortals were not supposed to posses the powers held within the stones."

"Where am I?" Nick whispered, trying to make a mental note of everything being said.

"You are in The Temple of the Phoenix. Or at least you are in some form," replied the voice.

"How did I get here?"

"It was thought that no mortal would ever be able to take the stones, and yet three did. There was a prophecy made by the guardian of the temple that one day a mortal with the blood of The Adventurer would find the secrets. The stones have the power to grant immortality to the holder. Somewhere in the world of the living at this very moment a man seeks to unite them and bring damnation to the world," continued the voice, ignoring Nick's question.

"I thought no mortal could posses the stones," Nick said, staring unblinkingly at the bird.

"For centuries the magic of the phoenix has prevented it. To slay an immortal creature enabled the spell to break," murmured the voice. "When the last phoenix is dead he will come for the stones."

Slowly the phoenix unfurled its wings and launched itself into the air. For a split second Nick saw the transparency of the bird as it hovered in front of him. It was a ghost.

"The stone that sits in the centre of the stone tablet, what does it represent?" Nick called as the bird turned and began to fly away.

"Death," the voice echoed as the bird faded away, leaving Nick in the darkness again.

"Nick?" a concerned voice asked distantly. In a rush everything flooded back to him, the ghostly phoenix shining brightly through the darkness in his mind.

"Death, it's death," he shouted as he sat up, his eyes flying open. Beside him he noticed the lantern Rose had been carrying earlier, resting by the central pillar. Sitting up he looked around for his own which lay broken and extinguished several feet away.

"W-what?" Rose asked, taken aback by his sudden outburst. She was sat on the dusty floor nearby, watching him closely.

"The stone that's missing," Nick said as he looked back at her. "The word you couldn't translate, it means death."

"Okay," she said slowly. "I'm not sure what that stone did to you but I doubt a bang to the back of your head made you any better at Latin."

"It was the phoenix," Nick said, determined to make her believe him.

"Maybe you should just lay back down," she whispered. As he looked down he saw the book in her hands.

"You think I've gone mad," he demanded. In a split second her eyes flashed to him, burning a darker blue. They always darkened when she got angry. Without saying a word she grabbed his shirt and pushed him down so that he was lying on the floor.

"Please, just leave it," she replied as calmly as she could manage before standing and walking towards the other side of the room.

"Why don't you believe me?" Nick asked quietly. For a moment she stayed silent, staring at the bookcase in front of her.

Pushing himself up, Nick clambered to his feet. The shock from the stone must have thrown him a lot further than he thought as he saw the stone column which marked the centre of the room a few feet away. Wincing for a moment he felt his head pound as he looked around, the light from the candles was faltering slightly.

Unsteady on his feet Nick made his way towards the desk that the stones stood on. As he drew closer the humming got louder. The buzzing seemed to penetrate his mind. Stopping in front of the desk he looked down at them. Before he could reach out to touch them again they stopped humming. Curious, he paused, watching as they slowly lifted out of their places. For a minute they hovered in the air, perfectly still.

Without warning the stones began to move, circling around some invisible central force that held them tightly together. Silently he watched them, awestruck by the sudden change.

"What did you do?" a quiet voice said behind him. Spinning round he found himself face to face with Rose. For a split second their eyes locked.

"I didn't do anything," he said defensively as he stepped aside so that he was no longer face to face with her. Watching her take a step closer she seemed to accept what he had said.

"If that missing stone represents death, how does it fit into the pattern?" Rose asked, gesturing to the empty central hole.

"Didn't that book you were reading explain it?"

"No, it's just a child's book. I'm sure it wouldn't start going on about the meaning and reasons behind the death stone," she replied after a moment. "Would you tell . . . your . . . little children stories about death?"

He allowed her question to hang in the air, empty and unanswered. As he thought about it he could see her point. For several long minutes they stood in silence, neither knowing what to say next.

"Will you tell me about what happened?" Rose asked quietly, looking across at Nick.

"I was standing in this strange place, it was too dark to make out anything," Nick began. "Out of the darkness this blue light appeared. When it got closer it was a bird, a phoenix. It called the place The Temple of the Phoenix."

"How do you know the last stone represents death?" she asked.

"The phoenix was a guardian of one of the stones, their magic was supposed to protect the stones from falling in to the hands of mortals." Nick continued, waving away her question. "When an adventurer found a way to kill the phoenix it broke the spell over the stone. It warned that someone is after the stones for the wrong reasons. With them he could turn the world into hell."

Dropping into silence once more they both watched the stones spinning, both of them occupied by their own thoughts. Looking down, Nick caught sight of the cut across his right palm. The blood had dried to his hand, tinting the skin a dark red. As they watched the stones began to slow, noiselessly dropping back into their places in the stone tablet.

"Isn't a phoenix supposed to be immortal?" Rose asked, glancing at Nick again.

"I thought so too," he replied. "I guess that's what makes the stones so powerful."

"Well, five of the stones are already here," she said. "That just leaves the other two to find."

"Even if we could find the others," Nick considered.

"What could kill a phoenix though?"

"I don't know what happened earlier with that sword," Rose said softly. "But whatever it was it felt evil, an abomination to existence."

"It's a sword, it doesn't have feelings," Nick said with a laugh. The thought that a piece of metal could have any knowledge of evil was beyond belief. "Whatever happened in that tunnel must have been affecting you at the time."

"You're the one who just told me you were transported to an ancient temple, where the ghost of a phoenix told you a bunch of stones could make people immortal," Rose argued back, trying to make him realise how ridiculous it all sounded. "I think it's all a fantasy. Someone read about the legend and got a little too carried away with it.

"Whatever you say," Nick replied. Reaching out he touched the ice stone again, preparing himself for another shock. When none came he closed his fingers around it, lifting it from its place on the tablet. In the light from the candles it sparkled as he examined it. Satisfied that nothing more was going to happen he returned it to its place. Looking down at his hand he saw the cut had gone; mysteriously healed as if there had never been anything there.

CHAPTER FOUR
THE PROPHECY OF THE PHOENIX

In the distance the sound of dripping water had returned. Silently Nick and Rose stood watching the motionless stones. Since they had returned to their places the humming had stopped. When it was evident that nothing else was going to happen Nick turned to face Rose.

"We should get out of here," he said quietly. "There's no way of telling how long we've been in these tunnels." For several minutes she didn't respond, her eyes still focused downward, gazing at the stones.

Before she could speak there was a shuffling sound from the depths of the tunnel. Turning they watched, waiting for the source of the sound to materialise. Nick felt Rose's sharp intake of breath beside him as a shadow fell across the entrance of the room. In the flickering light of the candles a man appeared, staring at them.

"What are you doing in here?" shouted the man, his hoarse voice echoing off the rough walls.

"I'm sorry, we were-" Nick began, only to be interrupted by Rose seconds later.

"It's my fault. We were just bringing back the book that you let me borrow," she said quickly. In the shadows, his face lifted slightly as he realised who it was.

Stepping out of the shadows his features became more visible. He was an inch or two shorter than Nick. His face chiselled with age, the bushy black beard peppered with silvery grey hairs. Behind the square, wire frame glasses his blue eyes were dark and tired, telling their own story of torment and pain.

"How did you know we were here?" Nick asked quietly as he looked at the dirty white shirt William was wearing.

"I heard a bang a while ago," he replied. "With my age I can't move as fast as I would like. Dare I ask what happened?"

"That was my fault, I touched one of the stones on the desk and got a shock off it," muttered Nick. Indicating the desk behind him he continued. "I thought you were taken by The Dark Movement."

"How curious," he whispered, taking one of the stones in his almost skeletal fingers. Briefly, William explained how he had been allowed back to Gladstow in return for future services that would be required.

With the insistence of William, Nick slowly recounted the story that he had already told Rose, careful not to skip any of the details. William's eyes widened in disbelief as Nick told him how the stones had risen from the tablet and started circling each other.

"There should be a book around here somewhere," William muttered, apparently speaking more to himself than the two before him.

Rose, who had taken to staring around the room as Nick talked, was itching to get out of the underground labyrinth. When William returned he held a battered, dust covered book in one hand. "Here it is."

Carefully prising the book open he searched for the right page. It amazed Nick how easily he could read the miniscule writing. After a minute he stopped turning pages and handed the book to Nick who began to read, Rose looking over his shoulder.

A time will come to pass a thousand years from now when a phoenix is slain by the seeker of The Immortality Stones. As the embers of the last of The Seven Phoenixes are extinguished the bond of immortality will be broken. The stones of air, earth, fire, ice, lava, water and death will be reunited, granting the power of immortality to evil.

Faith rests in the hands of The Saviour and a sword forged from the fires of a dying phoenix.

If he fails the world will forever be bathed in darkness and the blood of the innocent.

"Who wrote this?" Nick asked as he closed the book, holding it out to William.

"There was never an author's name on the cover. As far as the library in the city was concerned, it never existed," William said. "It's a shame that there is a page missing, it is a very good book if you want information about the myth.

"Are you saying that it's actually real then?" Rose butted in impatiently.

"The stones, the prophecy, it is all true!" William confirmed. "A sword forged in the fires of a dying phoenix, that bit I'm not so sure about."

"What makes you say that?" Nick asked curiously.

"No one has ever seen a phoenix," he replied. "Or at least they never told me."

"After I touched the stone I saw a phoenix," Nick reminded him. "How do you know the prophecy is true if you don't believe that the phoenix exists?"

"He is after the stones again," William whispered, determined not to say the name. "Right now as we stand here he searches all the locations where they were found."

"How could he have had them before?" Rose asked. "There are five of them sitting on the desk."

"Years ago, before he knew of the existence of the death stone he had all the others. When he tried to make himself immortal the spell backfired, ripping life from one half of his body while making the other half immortal," William explained. "His body and mind was torn with agony and he fled, leaving behind the stones. It was then that I collected the five on the desk behind you."

"What about the Lava stone?" Nick questioned.

"Lost, when I retrieved the others it was missing," William whispered. "How it happened I do not know but I believe that it returned to the cave where it was held since its creation."

"Is it still there?" Nick asked quickly. Out of the corner of his eye he could see Rose folding her arms across her chest and shuffling her feet impatiently.

"As far as I know, it is. When I went to retrieve it a few weeks back I-" William said, stopping abruptly when he heard a humming sound coming from behind Nick. Moving between them he looked down at the stones on the desk, Nick and Rose turning to face him.

"That was what drew us down here earlier," Nick muttered when he saw the stones.

"Curious, I've never heard them do that before," William said to the room in general. Moving next to William, Nick reached out and touched the fire stone which sat closest to him. As his skin came into contact with the surface the red stone began to glow slightly.

"That didn't happen last time," Nick whispered. Hearing a scratching sound he looked up to find William rifling through his book again.

"It's here, all here!" He cried triumphantly as he began to read, oblivious to the look Nick and Rose were sharing behind his back. Looking over William's shoulder he saw the words of the prophecy written on the page.

"I don't follow," Nick said as he read the lines of the prophecy through in his head again.

"It says that the stones will be reunited, granting the power of immortality to evil," William quoted from the book. "I believe that the prophecy refers to him. Since his failed attempt to harness the powers of the stones he has changed, moving beyond what could be called normal evil. As he searches for the stones he is ruthless in his attacks on the towns and villages he visits."

"That answers the first part, what about the second?" Rose enquired.

"Faith rests in the hands of The Saviour and a sword from the fires of a dying phoenix," William whispered. "It appears that our only hope of defeating the evil which is approaching lies with one person. As for the sword, it is like nothing that I have ever heard about. There are no drawings of it and no records of it except for its mention in this book.

"Well, at least the last part seems obvious," Nick muttered. "If The Saviour fails then nothing will stop him."

"Who is 'The Saviour' though?" Rose asked, looking towards William for the answers. So far he had supplied all of them.

"It doesn't matter," Nick interrupted. "If five of the stones are here then there is nothing he can do."

"From what I have seen here, I would hazard a guess that 'The Saviour' is you Nick," William said slowly. "Never have the stones reacted in such a way to the touch of a person. Combined with your vision of the phoenix it seems a reasonable conclusion.

"How can it be me?" Nick laughed as he looked at William in disbelief. "What have I ever done to get into this?"

"You haven't done anything," William consoled him. "Many years ago, when I was much younger I first heard the story of Immortalis Calx, The Immortality Stones to you. When I shared the tale with two friends they immediately caught on to what I was thinking, find the stones. They signed up for the adventure without a moment's hesitation.

The work was slow; it took us months of pouring over books in the library to find any hint of the legend. Finally we had it, this book, our guide to the depths of the story. We were young, naive; we thought if we found the stones we would share the powers between us."

"What happened?" Nick asked quietly, watching as Rose twiddled a lock of black hair around her finger.

"We were betrayed. Your grandfather and I were betrayed by him," William said with an air of loathing in his voice as he refused to use a name.

"How am I supposed to defeat him when I know almost no magic or how to fight properly with a sword?" Nick asked, still trying to get his head around the task that was being handed to him.

"I can teach you all that I know," William replied. "Hopefully it will be enough."

"What about Rose?" he asked after a moment.

Taking a minute to return the book he was holding to its place on the shelf William ignored Nick's question, ushering them in front of him as he guided them through the tunnels towards the exit and the surface. As they walked their conversations stretched to Nick's time in the city.

Almost an hour had passed since they had left the room containing the stones when they emerged from the trapdoor. Blinded momentarily, Nick realised it was just after sunrise. They had spent the whole night wandering through the underground tunnels.

Insisting that he would need to speak with Nick's parents before he could begin his training, William took the lead again. When asked what she was going to do, Rose just shrugged her shoulders sheepishly and continued to follow them. However, it was left to Nick to gently push the door open, hoping that his parents were still asleep.

In less than a second that hope was crushed when he opened the door to find his mother standing on the other side, hands on hips. With a scowl she grudgingly allowed them to enter when she saw that William was with them. Her eyes lingered slightly longer on Rose as she slipped inside after Nick.

Insistence from his mother forced William to take the seat by the fire, leaving Nick and Rose to sit on the floor. As she rushed around completing her morning routine she talked amiably with William about the latest events. When she disappeared outside to fetch some more wood Nick leaned towards Rose.

"What's wrong?" he asked quietly, trying to keep his voice low so that no one else would hear.

"Nothing," she whispered back. When Nick raised an eyebrow at her she crumbled. "Your mother hates me, did you see the look she gave me?"

"I don't hate you, dear," a voice said from the doorway before Nick could respond. Standing there was the woman in her late thirties, a small bunch of logs in her arms and a weak attempt at a smile passing over her lips.

"I'm sorry. I didn't realise you had returned," Rose apologised, her eyes falling to the floor in embarrassment.

"Now what was it you wanted to ask me about?" she said turning to William as she changed the topic to avoid the awkward silence that was building.

"You are aware of The Prophecy of the Phoenixes?" William asked as he watched Rose shuffle slightly closer to Nick.

"Of course I am," she replied. "After all the time my father-in-law spent cooped up in that old library with you and Rose's grandfather how could I not?"

"The other person was my grandfather?" Rose interrupted, her eyes flashing up in a heartbeat. "How could my grandfather have betrayed you? What did he do, hand over the stones to him?"

For a minute William looked at her in silence. Turning back to Nick's mother he decided to ignore her questions. There would be time for explanations later on. Slowly he began to explain his plans to her, continuously insisting that Nick would be in no danger.

"No," she said firmly. "Absolutely not."

For a little over half an hour William had explained what he had been able to deduce from the prophecy as well as all that Nick had told him. All the while Nick and Rose had remained silent except to bid Nick's father good morning when he had joined them by the fire.

"To me, it sounds like we need Nick," his father interjected as he wiped the last remnants of raspberry juice from his lips. "The stories that are passed around in the fields say that The Dark Movement is getting more powerful, gathering followers as he travels and killing those who won't join him."

"I still say that it is too dangerous for someone of his age," she argued back.

"Of course it will be dangerous, travellers and merchants both tell of how he has ruthlessly crushed towns and villages," he said calmly, placing a consoling hand on his wife's shoulder as he looked down at Nick and Rose. "If the prophecy is true, Nick may be the best shot at destroying that monster once and for all."

"You've already lost your father to this adventure and now you're willing to do the same to your son?" she whispered. Reaching up, she dabbed at her eyes with the fabric of her dress.

"I give you my word that I will do all I can to protect him and prepare him for what is to come," William said humbly. "I will meet with you Saturday morning," he added to Nick as he stood up. "Being a lot older now I will need some time to prepare."

"I'll see you later," Rose muttered to Nick. With a wave to his father she hurried after William, pausing momentarily to flash a smile in Nick's direction when she was certain that no one else was looking. Returning it he watched as the door swung shut behind her.

CHAPTER FIVE

THE MONKS OF AKRANEIMACY

As November began to draw to a close the fog and mist flowed down off the hills surrounding the Welsh English border, rolling in to the village of Gladstow. For two months now, Nick had been with William in the underground tunnels and rooms that the old man had constructed in his younger years.

It was the morning of 23rd November, a bitterly cold day, that William decided it was a suitable time to move Nick on to the more advanced stage of his training. For that he had been told he would require a staff.

"Morning Nick," William said brightly as the door opened and the seventeen year old stepped inside. Since he had returned from the company of The Dark Movement, the dark bags under his eyes had noticeably lessened.

"What are we working on today?" Nick asked as he released the steel sword that was sheathed at his waist before sitting opposite William at the small wooden desk.

Throughout the hours that the two of them had spent in the underground labyrinth, William had begun to teach him all that he would need to know, everything from the depths of the prophecy and the legends surrounding the stones. William had enchanted a sword to fight against Nick when he complained that he was too old to fight himself. So far it had proved to be extremely draining, both physically and mentally.

"I think that there is very little left for you to learn fighting against an enchanted sword," William replied. "There is a small piece in the books to look at, but we can save that for another day. Today I thought we would get your staff made so that we can move on to the magical side of things."

"Where will we get it from?" Nick commented curiously, getting to his feet as William did so.

"There is a small island in the North Atlantic that is home to The Monks of Akraneimacy," William explained. "On the island they tend to the tree that produces the wood we will use to make a staff."

Returning his sword to his waist, Nick watched as William shuffled around the cluttered room. With great difficulty he lifted down what looked like a stack of stone discs. Taking two from the top he placed them on the desk that he and Nick had been sitting at. With a long finger he began to trace out the name of the island, small fragments of stone chiselling away in to dust as the name became engraved in the tablet.

"Watch yourself when you land," William muttered, handing one of the stones to Nick. A small spray of green sparks surrounded Nick as he watched William place his palm over the stone before vanishing into thin air. Taking one last moment to look around at the daylight filled room, he placed his own hand over the centre of the disc.

Under his palm he felt the letters that William had carved grow warm and before he knew it he was surrounded by a whiteness that pressed against him. The feeling of vulnerability that so often came over him in these journeys enveloped him. One second he was in a blinding white light and then he was stumbling forward into knee deep snow, the bitterly cold wind whipping at his long hair.

"Come," bellowed William over the howling wind. Nick turned when he felt the old man's hand on his shoulder. William's hair had been blown wildly out of place, his beard splattered with snowflakes from the blizzard that circled around them. Eager to get out of the cold as quickly as possible, Nick hurried after him.

Together they forged a deep track through the snow down a slight incline. When the ground began to level out again, a dark structure became visible through the barrier of icy flakes. The relief Nick felt as the snow became shallower ran through his veins like fire, drawing warmth to the extremities that had become numb. As they drew closer, the heavy wooden door creaked open. A man appeared a split second later, waving them enthusiastically inside. Passing between two of the black basalt columns, which had formed in a hexagonal shape, they moved inside.

As he entered he felt a wave of warmth pass over him, instantly drying his clothes. In the light of the room Nick began to examine the man more closely. He wore a simple robe, the bottom reaching the ground and hiding his feet. On his chest, directly over his heart, a blue phoenix was stitched on the deep, fiery red material. What Nick assumed was the world, gripped in the phoenix's talons.

"He is the one?" asked the man quietly, looking to William for an answer while Nick stood uncomfortably on the fringe of the conversation.

"I believe so," William replied.

"The stories are true," cried the man jubilantly. "The Saviour has come at last." It was only now that Nick noticed the seven men gathered by the fire as they let out a triumphant cry, all of them rushing forwards. They were all dressed identically with long red robes, although none bore the blue phoenix on their chests. As he watched them, Nick noticed they all had similar dark brown or black hair that had been cut short. Their ages ranging considerably form one who looked only a couple of years older than Nick to a man who looked to be in his late fifties.

There was a brief round of introductions in which Nick and William shook hands with each of the men. All of them praised him as 'The Saviour', much to Nick's embarrassment. He felt like no saviour, it was only a prophecy from a thousand years ago that identified him as that.

"We are The Monks of Akraneimacy," said the man with the phoenix on his robe, who had identified himself as Infinitas. Behind him the others nodded feverishly. "Many years ago we were displaced from our sacred lands. Now that The Saviour has arrived we will return to our land and the evil spoken of in The Prophecy of the Seven Phoenixes will be banished."

"The Seven Phoenixes will return!" chorused the monks.

"I thought the phoenixes were killed," Nick said. "In the prophecy it says that the embers of the last of The Seven Phoenixes would be extinguished."

"There is a legend that tells us that The Seventh Prophecy of The Seven Phoenixes spoke of the return of The Seven Phoenixes from The Seven Worlds of the Dead-" began Infinitas who was cut off by the other monks chorusing 'Long live the Seven Phoenixes!'.

"Alas, the prophecy was lost long before we could record it," Infinitas continued with a disapproving look at the other monks.

"What do you mean lost?" Nick questioned.

"Lost in time," Infinitas replied. "The fifth piece also vanished around the same time. So the legend says anyway."

"Can we see the other pieces?" William interjected.

"They were stolen-"

"Stolen," echoed the monks. Infinitas sent a scalding look at them before he continued.

"Only the first prophecy remains. The book was taken and the rest torn-"

"Torn," repeated the monks in unison.

"Will you stop doing that," an irritated Infinitas said as he turned to them. Under his gaze they turned, scurrying back to the fire. A couple of them left a muttered apology hanging in the air as they hurried away.

"We need to get your staff, before the snow gets too deep," Infinitas said, waving a hand vaguely in the direction of something that was obscured by the black stone wall. "Curator, fetch our guests a thick robe each."

From the fireside, one of the younger looking monks rose to his feet. Quickly he moved to a wall where a group of long red robes hung on small individual pegs.

"We will accompany you to Sanctus Nemus, the tree from which we take the wood to make the staff," Infinitas said. Seeing what was happening, the other monks stood, gathering beside the door while William and Nick slipped their robes over the clothes they were already wearing.

As soon as they stepped back outside Nick knew that the robes had magic embedded deep in them. The bitter cold he had felt before in his body was gone, warmth surrounding all of his body that was covered by the cloak. Looking down, a phoenix that had been worked in to the fabric caught his eye.

The deep snow was making the walk hard but, doubled with the snow storm that swirled around them, it became near impossible. Ideas on why William had brought him here now chased each other round his mind like the snowflakes before his eyes. In the distance something large appeared out of the wall of snow. Drawing closer it took the shape of a tree, surrounded by pearly white stone pillars.

To Nick it felt truly bizarre to have all of the monks escorting them in some kind of mismatched guard of honour. Reaching out, Nick ran his finger tips over one of the stones. It was incredibly smooth, feeling almost like ice rather than rock.

Passing in to the centre of the circle there seemed to be a slight prickle in the air. He had felt the same sensation when he had returned to Gladstow.

"After an act of magic a trace is often left in the air," William said from somewhere behind him. Turning to his right, Nick saw the old man watching him intently, as if he had been reading his thoughts. Nick gave him an acknowledging nod before returning his gaze to the tree ahead of them. Infinitas had stopped beside it and now stood facing Nick, William and the other monks.

"The Sanctus Nemus was identified as magical shortly after it was discovered," he explained. "Beneath the snow, the roots of the tree wrap themselves around the rocks on which it grows. Not needing any soil in which to grow was the first indication of its powers.

Shortly after Senior Unus, the tree's discoverer removed a branch to examine its properties more closely. Within a week the branch that had been removed had re-grown, an exact replica of the one removed. Please, take your time to select a branch for your staff."

Not wanting to stay out in the snow any longer than necessary, Nick did a quick circle of the tree, his eyes scouring the bare branches. After several minutes he decided on a smooth, slightly curved branch and stood back to watch as Infinitas severed it from the tree.

Shaking off the snow that had settled on it he passed it to Nick, pausing to watch as a tiny green shoot sprouted from the spur.

"We will head back to the house to finish this," Infinitas said, drawing Nick's awestruck gaze away from the new branch that was beginning to grow.

They had barely taken a couple of steps when a loud crack echoed across the tiny barren island. On all sides, figures in dark grey cloaks appeared through the blizzard. Nick had hardly registered their presence when a bolt of red light streaked past him.

It may have been a reflex, or, merely because there was nothing more he could do, but Nick felt his hand diving for his waist, reaching for his sword.

"No," Curator said as he stopped Nick's hand before it could grasp the metal. "You run. Get back to the house, we will protect you." Without giving Nick any time to protest he turned, pulling a staff, which until now had gone unnoticed by Nick, from its holster on his back.

Out of the corner of his eye he saw a transparent green shield erupt into existence, deflecting another spell harmlessly out to sea. In a way that was reminiscent of his younger years, William grabbed Nick by the arm, dragging him through the thick snow as fast as he could. They didn't stop until they reached the wooden door to the house.

Turning back in the direction they had come they looked around for any sign of the monks. He heard it before he saw it. The sound of crackling magic drawing closer. Out of the whirlwind of snow a smoky black fork of light sped towards them. Paralyzed with fear all he could do was stand and watch.

In a split second, Nick found William pushing him into the snow bank beside the door with the agility of a man half his age. Snapping back to his senses he searched the air for the spell, watching as it hit the wall behind where he had been standing before. As it collided with the wall it exploded, showering them both with flaming pieces of basalt rock.

Without properly registering the pieces of white hot rock that were beginning to smoulder their way through the fabric of his cloak, he was hauled to his feet. Vaguely he felt himself forced through the door which slammed shut as he was joined by William. With his back against the wall, he allowed himself to slowly slide to the floor.

"What was that?" Nick asked, glancing up at William who stood over him.

"That was a killing spell," he replied after a moment.

"But I didn't hear anyone say an incantation," Nick said, speaking more to the room in general than William.

"The killing spell is not like other magic," William explained. "To kill is to violate the course of nature. All one needs to do is merely feel the desire to kill, the staff does the rest. That also explains the smoky appearance of the spell, without an incantation the spell becomes hollow. Maybe it is because it is not properly complete or that no one has a strong enough desire to kill to give it its full colour."

"What colour would it be if there was an . . . incantation," he asked.

"Imagine the night sky with no moon, no stars. The perfect black. That is the true colour of a killing spell," William said, his voice bitter with the hatred of the topic they were discussing. "Only one person is said to have ever produced a true killing spell."

"Numquam," Nick muttered. Glancing up he saw William's confirming nod. "I have to kill him don't I."

"One day yes, you will have to kill him."

"I don't think I could ever have that desire to kill anyone, not even him," Nick whispered as he pushed himself back to his feet.

"There is more than one way to kill a man," William said. "When the time arrives you will be able to do what you need to."

"You think it will be the sword?" Nick questioned as he walked over to the fire. For the several minutes that they both stood in silence, Nick stared into the heart of the fire, watching as the tongues of flame wrapped themselves around the charred wood.

"If the sword does exist," William said. "Then I believe that it will be the weapon to finally banish this man . . . this monster." Falling into silence they waited for the monks to return.

Almost an hour had passed before the door opened again. As Infinitas entered, Nick saw that his face was plagued with concern. Several more minutes passed before six of the other monks entered, carrying something large between them. It was seconds later, as the monks drew closer, that Nick felt his stomach drop as he realised they were carrying one of their own. One of their brothers.

"You couldn't have done anything," Infinitas said consolingly as if he had seen the dark look in Nick's eyes before. Anger he didn't even know existed inside of him burst out.

"I could have at least tried, he told us to run, to hide!" Nick shouted, uncaring that the other monks stopped to stare at him. "If I'm supposed to be The Saviour why couldn't I have saved him? Why stop me fighting if I'm supposed to be the one to end all of this?"

"The time is not right for you to fight yet," Infinitas said unflinchingly.

"What the hell is that supposed to mean?" Nick argued, determined to get answers as he took a step towards Infinitas.

"There will be a time when you need to fight, that time is not now," William said as he stepped between them.

"So I'm just supposed to sit around and wait until some prophecy from a thousand years ago tells me it's the right time?" Nick demanded. "Innocent people are dying and you won't let me do anything."

"Yes," Infinitas and William said together.

"Curator gave his life to make sure you are still alive to fight your battle," Salus said quietly as he stepped forward. Of all the monks he was the youngest, and yet the cuts and scars told a different story. One of a battle worn man who had seen the horrors that evil was unleashing on towns and villages.

A wave of guilt crashed over Nick like a waterfall. Had he been so single-minded that he did not recognise the sacrifice Curator had made? He was throwing a tantrum like a young child. Maybe they were right about him not being ready.

"For years our job has been to find The Saviour and protect him from harm so that on the final day evil can be defeated." Infinitas added as he watched the anger fading from Nick, and William shuffled his feet uncomfortably.

After a few minutes of accepting silence, Infinitas held out his hand, taking the branch that Nick had chosen. When they had all gathered around the fire he began to carve and shape the wood with his hands, the scrapings falling into the flames. As the chippings burnt, small purple sparks fluttered out of the wood, crackling quietly.

Finally Infinitas lay down Nick's now fully carved staff. Throughout the time they had sat huddled around the fire all of the monks had been silent. It may have been out of respect for their friend and Nick was not going to disrupt their mourning, he already felt bad enough after his earlier outburst.

All of them turned as one when Infinitas stood, eight pairs of eyes following him as he walked across the stone floor to one of the walls. Gently he opened the doors of a wooden cabinet and reached inside. From where Nick was sitting it appeared to be empty so it was not until Infinitas returned that he saw what had been inside.

Held delicately in both hands was a miniature figure of a phoenix, cast out of gold. Silently he fixed the figurine to the wooden ball of the staff, in such a way that the claws of the phoenix gripped it. Down the length of the staff tiny shapes were carved into the wood, their symbolic nature remaining unknown to Nick. Certain that it was now securely attached Infinitas handed the staff to its new owner.

Taking it in his hands he felt the wood warm slightly as he held it, his eyes lingering momentarily on the golden phoenix as its eyes seemed to sparkle in the fire light.

"Each of the eyes are made of a single diamond," Infinitas explained as he watched Nick focusing on the phoenix. "The legend that accompanies it says that there is a diamond embedded in the hilt of a sword to complete the trio of perfect diamonds. Each diamond representing one of the three souls a phoenix is said to have."

"How does that work?" Nick asked quietly, still awestruck by the beauty of the golden phoenix.

"A phoenix has three souls; each time it uses its tears to save a life it gives away one of those souls," Infinitas began. "When it has given away all three of its souls it will burst into flames, rising from the ashes reborn. So the legend goes; a phoenix magically attached one of its souls to a diamond that resides in the hilt of a sword. The two diamonds on this figurine are supposed to represent the other two souls the phoenix gave away before it died."

"How could it die though?"

"Normally when a phoenix saves a life with its tears it gives away the soul, but by binding one to a diamond the soul was still bound to this world. As it was no longer part of the phoenix, the phoenix could not survive without a soul which caused it to burst in to flames. However, it could not be reborn as the soul that still belonged to it was still out there."

"So the phoenix was stuck between death and rebirth?" Nick asked as he tried to work it through in his head to make sense of it.

"Essentially, yes." Infinitas confirmed. "Although I doubt that the sword really exists, it is, in the end, just a legend told to children."

Committing it to memory for later, Nick looked around at the others who sat by the fire. All of the monks seemed to be deep in thought, William scratching at his beard as he sat beside Nick contemplating what Infinitas had said. With a stifled yawn he stretched. At some point he had lost track of the time and was left wondering how long they had been on the island.

Thanking the monks for their help and with sympathetic apologies for the loss of their friend, Nick and William headed outside. At the insistence of Infinitas they had kept their robes on and were now thankful for the warmth as they inched through the deep snow.

For several minutes they walked in silence, the darkness beginning to press in on them. Out of nowhere William had produced two stone discs, identical to those that they had used to travel to the island.

"We should be fine travelling from here," he shouted over the sound of the wind and the waves that crashed against the rocks. Handing one of them to Nick, he disappeared, lost in a flurry of green sparks and snow. Taking one last breath of the bitterly cold air Nick looked around. The house belonging to the monks had long since disappeared behind a thick blanket of snow. Placing his palm over the centre of the disc he caught one last glimpse of the snow covered island before he was enveloped in whiteness again.

CHAPTER SIX
ROSE'S STORY

Still trying to come to terms with what had happened on the tiny island the previous day, Nick found himself wandering through the centre of the village. Neither Nick nor William had discussed the events when they returned; merely bidding each other farewell, saying that they would meet again the next morning. That hadn't happened.

It was almost midday now. When Nick had arrived at William's house he had found the door locked. Having had no response when he knocked on the door he had given up, assuming that the old man had something more important to be doing. Since then he had wandered through the narrow streets, heading in no particular direction.

Pausing in the square he took a moment to run his fingertips across the weathered stone in the centre, thinking of the night he and Rose had discovered the network of caves under the village. Hearing someone shouting his head snapped up, searching for the source. Seeing no one around his curiosity got the better of him and he set off, following the sound of the voices.

Stopping just around the corner he listened. The shouting had stopped, replaced by the sound of a door slamming shut. Leaning around the side of the house to get a better view he collided with Rose.

"Sorry," she mumbled. Rubbing her shoulder she stepped around him and carried on walking as quickly as she could. Bewildered by her behaviour, he set off after her.

By the time Nick reached the village square again she had disappeared down one of the side streets. Running a hand through his hair he stopped, considering all the places she could possibly have gone. If she was in a bad mood she would normally head for the forest. That seemed like his best bet right now.

Walking as fast as he could without running he headed for the hilltop forest. The gentle breeze blowing from the north nipped at the bare skin on his neck and arms, forcing the hairs on his arms to stand up. Everything that had happened the day before lay discarded in the corner of his mind as he tried to remember what he had heard of Rose's shouting match.

The forest was almost silent; occasionally the sound of birds would break the peacefulness. Leaves that had been tossed aside by the trees no longer willing to support them littered the ground. Crunching beneath his feet, the carpet of copper brown leaves were enough to give away his presence to anyone listening hard enough.

Unsure where he would find Rose, Nick wandered aimlessly between the trees, straining to hear the smallest sound. Several times he had spun round at the slightest sound only to find a startled creature scurrying for safety deeper in the forest.

Hearing what sounded like a whimper he froze to the spot, slowly scanning the trees for the source. Finding nothing he waited a minute longer. When he heard it a second time he looked around, higher this time.

Sitting on a low knotty oak branch was Rose, her legs swinging over the side with her back to him. Quietly he approached her, unsure what to say. On the trunk of the tree he noticed the letters NH and RH etched into the bark. Judging by the movement of her hand she was carving something into the bark now.

"Rose?" Nick said quietly. When she didn't respond he ducked under the branch so that he was in front of her. Before he could see what she had been carving she covered it, twisting round so that her back was to him again. "Please tell me what's wrong."

"You wouldn't understand," she replied in what was barely above a whisper.

"I still want you to tell me though," Nick said, leaning against the branch beside her. When she glanced down at him, he saw the tears in her eyes.

"Fine," she mumbled through her sleeve as she wiped away the tears. "While you were away yesterday my father disappeared. My mother blames me."

"Why?"

"She thinks that he disappeared because of all the time I spend with you and all the strange stuff that seems to revolve around you," Rose replied.

"We've hardly spent any time together lately," Nick commented.

"I know, that's what we were arguing about," Rose said quietly.

"I'm sure everything is going to be fine," he replied, pulling himself up on to the branch to sit beside her. She managed to muster a weak smile before looking back at her feet. Letting her head rest on his shoulder he watched as she closed her eyes.

"What's going to happen with all of this prophecy stuff?" she asked.

"Honestly, I don't know," he said. "If I knew I would tell you." For several minutes they both fell silent.

"And after?"

"I haven't thought about it, for all we know there may not be an after," Nick said as he eased her head off his shoulder so he could jump down. When he stood facing her he continued. "The prophecy doesn't give us any clues that it will be a happy ending." Moving her hand across, he tried to get a glimpse of what she had been carving. Before he could register any of what he saw, he felt her foot against his chest, pushing him back gently.

"No," she said when he looked up at her questioningly. Deciding now was not the best time to argue, he helped her down from the branch.

"Is there anything else you want to talk about?" he asked, gesturing for her to walk with him.

"I'm just worried about you," she replied sheepishly. "All the stories about the towns and villages he's destroyed. Those he's killed when they wouldn't join him.

"I thought you knew this was going to be dangerous from the start though," he said as they walked off the path, weaving in and out of the old trees.

"You remember the night we found the stones, when you woke up I was reading a book," Rose said. "There was a poem in there; it was related to the stones in some way. It just scared me." Reaching into a pocket she produced a piece of paper which looked as if it had been torn from a book. The page had turned a faded yellow, the ink that traced out the letters cracked and flaking. Pausing beneath one of the smaller trees he took it from her as she held it out to him. He noticed that she was watching as he began to read, studying his face as if she was expecting a reaction similar to the fear she had.

Seven prophecies are set to be completed,
an ancient ritual by seven monks will be repeated
Through seven worlds of the dead, there shall rise,
seven shadows returning from the skies
On the seven paths carved of stone,
the seven phoenixes will reclaim their throne
Now seven stones that once were lost, reunite,
granted immortality, evil will rise to the highest height
Eternity of air, earth, fire, ice, lava, water and death,
after the final battle only one will take breath
Heroes born to the sons of those betrayed,
seeking a diary on a body decayed
Encased in this poem for children,
the location for final hope is hidden
Nowhere to run, nowhere to hide,
a third will have to choose their side
Guided by the hand of fate,
raised to see the world they helped create

Every path leads to a single place,
and on the longest day, good and evil meet face to face

"We already knew this from the prophecy," Nick said, unsure what he was supposed to see in it. Folding the page back up, he held it out to her.

"Didn't you see it? 'Heroes born to the sons of those betrayed'," she asked. "Heroes, it means there is more than one. You don't have to do this on your own."

"It's a poem for children, it even says so itself," Nick pointed out. He had a vague idea of the direction this was heading.

"Why won't you let me help?" she said

"One person has already died to protect me," he replied. "I don't want there being any more, especially not people I'm close to."

"What about me? What if something happens to you?"

"You know I can't promise anything," he answered. "I will be as careful as I can." Before she had a chance to argue back there was a soft scratching noise ahead of them. In an instant both of them froze, searching for the source.

Out from between two oak trees hopped a bird, bearing a slight resemblance to a rooster. With feathers that faded from dark green to black its tail feathers stood out, a blistering white against the fallen leaves. For several seconds it scratched around with the claws at the end of its slender black legs before looking up at Nick and Rose.

Sparing each other a bewildered glance they looked back just in time to see the bird tilt its head to one side. Expecting it to spread its dark wings and fly away, Nick took a step closer for a better look. To his surprise it stayed where it was. Slowly he approached it, reaching out to try and touch it even though he was still ten feet away from it. Quietly it clicked its black beak, its eyes appearing white as it shifted backwards into a small patch of sunlight filtering through the trees. When it stopped he saw a worm wriggling, clamped in the bird's vicelike beak.

Behind him he could hear Rose moving closer so that she stood beside him, her eyes focused on the strange bird as it began to hop away. Watching it move away Nick felt an irresistible urge to follow after it, discover where it had come from. With Rose behind him, he began to move after it, its white tail feathers flitting in and out of view as it moved over the leaves.

For several minutes they continued their pursuit before they emerged in a frosty hollow. In the shadows of the trees the grass was almost nonexistent, dust-like soil replacing it. In the centre, the bird was scratching at something that was lying on the ground.

Cautiously he approached, Rose hovering on the edge of the clearing. The first thing he noticed were the eyes, blank and vacant of life, and then the blood. Using its beak, the bird began to tear at the fleshy carcass of the young deer. On the dark feathers he could see half-dried blood stains. Sunlight, reflected off the hilt of his sword as Nick moved forwards, flashed across the eyes of the bird.

Startled, the bird thrust its wings open and took flight. As it flew towards the tree line a fiery circle erupted into existence, swallowing the bird. Disappearing with a crack all that was left behind was one of the white tail feathers of the bird. Looking back over his shoulder he saw Rose still hovering by the trees, her eyes unfocusedly staring at the dead deer.

Moving around the deer to avoid the blood, Nick walked slowly towards the fallen feather. Crouching down beside it he reached out to touch it, part of him expecting something to happen. But nothing did. The white feather just continued to lie there motionlessly.

"Did that bird kill the deer?" Rose asked when Nick returned to her, the white feather held limply in one hand.

"I don't think so, we were following it," Nick answered as they turned back into the forest. "There wouldn't have been enough time for it to do that."

For a while they walked in silence between the trees, heading back in the direction they had come. Nick was running the feather absentmindedly through his finger tips as he followed Rose. It didn't feel like a normal feather. Drawing his fingertips to the end of the feather again, he felt a sharp pain.

Looking down he saw a small trickle of blood dripping from a hairline cut across his finger. On the very tip of the feather a small amount of his blood clashed with the white of the feather. He watched as the blood began to disappear, as if it was being absorbed by the feather. Deciding not to mention it to Rose he continued in silence.

Having left the forest and returned to the village, Nick and Rose set about finding William. Their first choice, his house, rewarded them when the door opened just seconds after they had knocked. Replacing the door was a tired and weary looking William. The bags under his eyes had returned.

"Nick, I'm sorry about this morning," William said. "I had something I needed to check."

"That's alright. We have something for you to take a look at anyway," Nick replied, holding the feather out to William. Carefully he took it from Nick, examining it closely for a minute.

"Where did you get this?" William demanded, looking between Nick and Rose.

"The forest, it fell out of the tail of a bird as it flew off," Rose answered before Nick could open his mouth to respond.

"Tell me what happened. Everything."

For ten minutes they explained how they had first seen the bird and how it had led them to the clearing with the deer.

" . . . that was when it took flight and flew into a fiery oval shape and disappeared. The feather was all that was left behind," Nick concluded.

"Interesting, this may prove very useful!" William said excitedly as he rolled the feather between his fingers. "I will need some time to examine the feather more closely though."

"Do you know what bird the feather belongs to?" Rose asked.

"I have only ever seen one like this before but that was many years ago," he replied.

"What does it mean?" asked Nick, aware of Rose pulling her hair back beside him.

"As of now, I'm not sure," William said. "Once I have had more time to examine it I will be able to tell you more, hopefully."

"Is there anything I can do to help?" Nick questioned, desperate to know what relevance the feather had.

"There is something actually," he replied. "For the spell to work properly I need several hairs from a lynx. Five should do it," he added, checking the details in a small red leather covered book he had pulled from a shelf behind him. "It says that for the best results the hairs need to be collected during hours of darkness."

"Where would I find a lynx though?" Nick asked thoughtfully.

"I believe that one may be living in the forest outside the village. For several nights now I have heard its soft cry when I have been harvesting other ingredients," William explained.

"How am I supposed to get the hairs though? I don't think it would be too happy if I just pulled them out," Nick said sceptically.

"On the edge of the forest there is a type of fern, its leaves a slightly darker green than normal. With a gentle warming spell it gives off a strong scent," he continued. "If you offer the ferns to the lynx then the scent should be strong enough to pacify it while you take the hairs."

Nick and Rose watched as he dropped the book on to the table, turning, and walking towards a jug of water that stood on the side. Pouring some of the water into a small bowl he returned to the table, placing the bowl in front of Nick.

"Place your hand over the bowl, just above the surface of the water," he directed Nick. "I want you to imagine that the water is heating up, that you can feel the heat on your skin. Are you doing that?"

Nick did not reply, just gave a slight nod of his head as he kept his focus on the bowl of water. Giving him a moment to regain his full focus, William waited silently.

"Right, now say the incantation; Parum Estus."

"Parum Estus," Nick repeated as he watched the water, straining to feel the heat on his skin. Disappointed, he dropped his hand back to his side when the water didn't change.

With the encouragement of William he tried again only to yield the same result. However, on the sixth attempt he felt the tiniest increase in heat.

After almost twenty more minutes of practice, William was satisfied that heating the fern leaves would no longer pose a problem. Happy with his progress the only thing left worrying Nick was where to find the lynx.

"Where would be the best place to find the lynx?" Nick asked as William returned the water to its jug. Rose looked up momentarily from her place by the bookshelf. While Nick had been working on the warming spell, she had been looking through one of the books. As Rose buried her nose back in the book, Nick looked away.

"You will need to go deep into the forest," he advised. "The best place to look would be in the deep undergrowth, although it may wander a little distance if it is out hunting."

In his mind, Nick had a vague idea of where he would search first. Knowing that William was relying on him only served to increase the pressure of finding the lynx.

"What should I do if the ferns don't work?" Nick asked quietly, dreading the answer. For several long seconds he paused in thought.

"In that situation," William replied. "The best idea would be to run. Or you could stay and fight, but that wouldn't be advisable."

Slightly unnerved by William's answer, Nick left the old man to prepare the rest of the items he needed. With no other questions to ask Nick and Rose left the house, Rose trailing behind him, her nose still buried in the book William had let her borrow.

When they reached the village square they went their separate ways. Nick heading home to prepare for the night ahead and Rose leaving to try and persuade her mother to let her back in.

Chapter Seven
BETWEEN THE TREES

Just after ten that night Nick bid his parents farewell as, with lantern in one hand and a fish hanging limply in the other, he stepped outside. The darkness was silent this night as he walked towards the village square. When he arrived there he heard the sound of people talking. In the end his curiosity got the better of him and he decided to delay slightly his search for the lynx. Creeping quietly to the corner of the next house, he peered round.

In a shadowy corner of the street two men stood talking, one Nick recognised to be William. Edging out he tried to get a better view of the second man. The shadows fell across the man's face, making it impossible to identify him without getting any closer and risking exposure. Through his strained eyes he caught a glimpse of something white. Twiddling between two fingers he saw the white feather in William's hand.

Keeping to the shadows he sidled away, making almost no noise whatsoever. The rest of the village was silent except for the occasional sound of a night bird in the distance.

His walk towards the forest was lonely, his senses heightened in an attempt to penetrate the darkness further than the light cast by the lantern. Occasionally he would freeze; his head flicking in the direction of what he had thought was movement. He had never felt so alone, so isolated, and yet he forced himself on towards the tree line.

Not once did he look back at the village, not until he stood at the side of the first tree. In the darkness he could just about make out the shape of the village, resting peacefully in the blackness. Beyond that the lake looked like black velvet, reflecting the pinpricks of light from the stars. There was no moon hanging in the sky to show him anything beyond that, not that anyone would ever dare to go near the forest at night.

Every child had been told the tale about the whispers in the forest. Occasionally residents would say they heard strange noises filtering out from between the trees. The residents were well inclined to avoid the area at night. Some thought it to be a creature that would never show itself. Others believed the old trees held the souls of those they had lost to the other side.

Those views had become wildly distorted through time as people claimed to have seen a large, shadowy creature pawing at the few blades of grass close to the trees. The few who had seen it had been shunned, views towards them tending to the belief that they were either insane, or in more recent years, drunk. Eventually, after decades of discussion and arguments it had been put down as a fox or a small deer.

Almost three years ago, in the February of 1896, one of the villagers had returned on a dark night claiming to have seen a lynx out by the forest. Whether it was true or not, no one knew. Clearly William had believed the man. Now, as Nick moved beyond the tree line his eyes scanned the pathway, his ears pricking up, straining for the tiniest sound.

It was not long after he had entered the forest that he came across a small clump of the dark green ferns. The ones William had described to him. Placing the lantern down on the ground he crouched down, withdrawing a small pocketknife. One by one he began to cut at the stems of the ferns with the blunt blade.

Ten minutes after he had set to work on the ferns he stood up, a small clump in his hand. Stretching out the stiffness in his legs he looked around. Every direction looked identical. In his mind he tried to retrace his steps, still coming to the same conclusion; he was completely lost. Deciding that it was better to start searching than trying to figure out where he was he set off, hoping that he was going in the right direction.

For what felt like hours Nick walked through the dark forest, there was still no sign of the lynx or any creature for that matter. When he had stumbled across the small clearing he had decided to wait there. He had no idea why, but, somewhere in his subconscious it seemed like a good place to start.

At a complete loss to where the carcass of the deer had gone, he settled down in the undergrowth. Watching the spot where he had placed the cut up pieces of fish, he waited.

He had waited for so long that when he finally saw something he thought he had gone mad. In the centre of the clearing a small piece of fish was moving across the ground. Looking up, the trees were still and silent. There was nothing else in the clearing.

Taking hold of the handle of the lantern he picked up the ferns as well and stepped forward. Whatever was attacking the pieces of fish, it was invisible to him.

As he approached the pieces of fish continued to move. Whatever was there was oblivious to his presence. Under his foot he felt a stray twig crack. In the silence of the night the crack echoed. Even though he couldn't see it he felt the creature freeze.

Before him the creature materialised slowly.

On its body the slick black fur sat completely flat. Patterns of a lighter creamy fur covered its chest, stretching on to its stomach. At the tips of its ears a small tuft of black hair stuck up.

Almost the size of a small deer he recognised it as the mysterious lynx. Quickly, Nick began to back away as the lynx's head turned. In their sockets the eyes were tinted a burning red. Fumbling to get a proper grip on the fern leaves he dropped the lantern. In a second the candle light inside was extinguished and the lynx seemed to hesitate.

"Parum Estus," Nick muttered, hurriedly trying to warm the fern leaves.

For a moment the only thing that seemed to happen was the lynx drawing closer. Holding the ferns out in front of him he watched as the lynx slowed, sinking to the floor before it could get to him.

Plunged into almost complete darkness, Nick stopped backing away. Allowing his racing heart to slow to something that resembled a regular beat, he placed the ferns close to the lynx, setting about the search for his extinguished lantern.

After stumbling around the dark clearing for five minutes he found it smashed, the candle inside twisted and broken. With a set of matches that he had drawn from a pocket, he relit the candle.

How long he had been in the forest he no longer knew. What looked like sunlight was breaking into the sky above the clearing. Discarding that thought for later, Nick hurried back to the lynx that was slumped on the floor asleep. With no idea how long the effect of the ferns would last, he set about gathering the hairs.

All the while he did not dare let his eyes wander from those of the lynx. Carefully he pulled several of the creamy hairs from its chest. Beneath his touch, the lynx quivered, slowly waking from the fern induced sleep.

Scrambling, Nick struggled to gain his footing as he tried to back away. The lynx began to stretch as it rolled over to stand up.

"Not good," Nick muttered as the lynx's head snapped in his direction. "Really not good," he added as the lynx snapped its jaws at him.

There was no way that he could see to get past the lynx to the small crumpled pile of ferns that lay discarded, cold and useless. As the lynx drew closer every instinct was telling him to run for his life, and yet his legs were no longer cooperating with his mind.

When the lynx began to hiss and spit at him he came to his senses. Turning, he ran, blindly stumbling on the uneven ground as the candle dropped to the ground behind him. The sound of the lynx racing after him was the only sound that met his ears.

Ducking and diving between the trees he tried to put as much space as possible between himself and the pursuing lynx. He was certain that the ferns must still be having an affect otherwise, he was sure he would have been dead by now. His train of thought was lost when voices from up ahead made him stop.

Throwing himself behind a tree he felt his breath catch. Not a single fibre in his body twitched as he watched the lynx race past, heading straight into the clearing ahead.

Creeping closer, Nick peered through the darkness. The small hollow was engulfed in light from a single source. A group of cloaked figures stood, huddled around a fire. The lynx was almost upon them before they became aware of its presence.

In an instant they split apart as the lynx jumped at one of the cloaked figures, taking them down to the ground. Cries of agony from underneath the hood ripped through the silence as it tore at the cloak, searching for the flesh beneath it.

As the blistering light of a new day broke over the hollow Nick heard, for the second time in his life the crackling of a killing spell.

When the blinding light faded and Nick could see once more, the cloaked figure was climbing to its feet again, long rips and what looked like blood on the cloak. At the base of one of the great oak trees lay the body of the lynx, lifeless and unmoving.

The cloaked figures regrouped by the fireside and as they did so, Nick felt eyes fall across the place where he stood in the shadows but nothing happened. No shouts from those who had gathered, no killing spell that had made such easy work of the lynx came his way. Instead they resumed their conversation, allowing Nick to silently return to the darkness of the forest. Just before they fell out of sight he saw a fiery orange oval appear and the first of the figures disappear through it.

Light from the early morning sun was just enough to reveal the path before him. Upturned roots littered the path, waiting eagerly to bring him down to the ground to join them.

A new day had dawned and the sun hung low in the sky as Nick returned to the village. At some point in the darkness he had lost track of how far he had walked. Wearily he stumbled towards the village square, making in the direction of William's house, the only thing on his mind, sleep.

Turning the corner to William's house he saw the door creak open, William's tired eyes peering from behind his glasses. When he saw Nick his face relaxed a shadow of relief crossing it. It appeared that Nick wasn't the only one who hadn't had any sleep.

"You have the hairs?" asked William quietly, beckoning Nick inside. The room was dimly lit, all the curtains still closed and the candles all but flickering stubs.

"Yes," Nick replied, holding out the small collection of hairs.

"Fantastic," William said enthusiastically as he hurried over to his desk with the hairs. Curious, Nick followed him, noticing the tail feather twiddling between William's long fingers. "You must be tired. It has been a long night for both of us I feel. This should only take a few minutes and then I can let you get some rest."

Standing on the opposite side of the desk, Nick watched William close his eyes, muttering something incoherent under his breath. One by one he let the lynx hairs drop into the bowl of yellow liquid. In seconds the liquid began to bubble ferociously, giving off a distinct sulphuric odour.

As the tip of the feather pierced the surface of the liquid it began to crackle, fiery sparks seemingly jumping off the surface and fluttering away. Before he could register anything, Nick felt a hand seize the back of his neck, throwing him forwards towards the bowl. Then there was nothing.

Inside him he felt his lungs contracting, almost forcing him to breath in the sulphuric air that encased him. When he couldn't take it any longer he opened his mouth, the acidic taste blistering across his tongue, down his throat and through his lungs. Gasping for clean air he collided with something solid, the murky darkness slowly clearing.

Lying perfectly still he clamped his eyes shut, allowing his other senses to explore the area for him. There was something beneath him, rock, he thought as he felt a sharp edge pressing against his stomach. The smell of sulphur was still in the air, nowhere near as strong but there none the less.

Opening his eyes a crack he looked up. William was lying sprawled on the rocky ground a few feet away. Massaging the back of his neck he looked around. The ground was coated in a fine red dust, the rocks no exception to the odd colouring.

Carefully he clambered to his feet, stumbling slightly as his knees threatened to buckle beneath him. Looking around him he saw a fiery oval, similar in every aspect except size to the one he had seen when the bird had disappeared. A hand on his shoulder caused him to spin round.

"We need to leave here, now!" William rasped, a somewhat vacant look in his eyes. As he turned to face the portal again it disappeared. Leaving behind a cluster of sparks that fluttered harmlessly to the ground and a loud crack that resonated across the barren rock.

Looking to the skies, as if to ask for help, Nick expected to see the familiar watery canvas. Not here. Wherever they were it was anything but normal. The skies were no longer the deep blue he had always known, instead they were burnt orange, like the depths of a flame.

At the edge of the rocky island Nick prayed to see water that would bring back some semblance of normality. Once again his hopes were dashed, the water that should have been there replaced by slowly flowing lava. His first thought was to laugh at how ridiculous this place was, as if it was part of a dream. This was real, he concluded, pinching his arm for proof.

"Where are we?" Nick asked quietly, looking to William in expectation that the wise old man would know something.

"A place we should not be in," he replied cryptically. "We need to find a way out of here and fast."

"Why? What's going to happen?" Nick said, trying to hide the fear in his voice.

"They will find us," William said." Then he will come for us."

"Who will find us? Who will come for us?" Nick demanded, wishing that William would be straight with him and that he could help to quell the anxiety inside him.

"His creatures will find us and then he will come for us," William replied, panic beginning to ebb into his voice.

"You mean Num-"

"Do not say his name! Not here," William shouted. "He will only find us quicker then.

Deciding not to press the matter any further, Nick hurried after William who had made off in the opposite direction. There was still a feeling in the pit of his stomach that William wasn't quite telling him everything. Looking out over the lava ocean he saw another island. In the centre was a large black mass, bearing some resemblance to a castle.

Not daring to move too close to the edge of the rock, he looked over the edge. The lava was slowly rolling along beside them. If Numquam's creatures were trying to find them it was best to stick together, he mused, as he jogged to catch up with William.

Unsurprisingly William didn't acknowledge his presence; he seemed more focused on other things. What that was, Nick was not going to ask as he considered what the old man had previously said.

"What creatures would he send to find us?" Nick asked curiously, trying to break the silence.

"That bird you saw in the forest must be around here somewhere or we would not have been brought here," William replied sharply. "I don't know about anything else."

Nick had never thought to ask William about what had happened when he was taken by The Dark Movement. Was the reason for his panic that he had been here before? Did he already know how to escape from this place?

Before Nick could ask any of the questions that were rushing to the front of his mind, William stopped, freezing in his tracks as if he had been turned to stone. Scanning the landscape, he searched for the reason they had stopped.

Up ahead of them stood a tree, dead and leafless, the bark blackened. On the topmost branch sat a bird with white tail feathers that twitched as it cast its gaze in their direction. Nick recognised it as the one he had seen in the forest, the forest that now felt so far away, almost a part of another world.

From its vantage point in the tree that stood atop a small, rocky mound the bird watched them. Nick could feel its gaze on him, as if it had recognised him as he had recognised it. Out of the corner of his eye Nick saw movement.

"Get down," said William, pulling Nick behind a large boulder with him.

"What was it?" Nick asked quietly, peering round the side of the rock to search for what he had seen.

"A group of black panthers, I just hope they are blind like the other creatures in this place." William replied.

"But the bird can't be blind, it was looking directly at me," Nick contradicted. Somewhere in the back of his mind he found himself laughing. If they were on an island surrounded by lava, how did the panthers get here?

"That bird is not a creature of this place," he said. "It is not bound by the same forces as the panthers."

"Then what is that bird? Where does it come from?" Nick asked as he heard rock sliding over rock. William did not reply.

When Nick turned to ask him again he saw why. William was frozen to the spot, hardly daring to breath as one of the panthers sniffed at him. Holding his breath he watched the panther.

The sockets that should have held eyes only contained what looked like bloody scabs. Otherwise it looked completely normal, its short black fur gleaming in the light of the red sky. Snarling at William, the panther revealed a set of razor sharp teeth. Certain that a particularly painful end was on its way Nick screwed his eyes closed.

No claws tore at his skin, no teeth ripped at his exposed flesh. For a second he allowed himself to squint through his eyelashes, searching for the panther. The creature had stopped sniffing at William and moved past them. As he watched it sauntering along beside the lava it paused to sniff at one of the red rocks. Looking across at William, they both breathed a heavy sigh of relief.

Feeling something warm against his neck Nick lifted a hand, reaching to feel what it was. When his fingertips came into contact with something soft he froze.

Turning his head slowly he saw black fur. One of the panthers was sat on top of the rock, its nose only a couple of inches from his neck. As it growled quietly he pulled his hand away slowly. Looking towards William for help he saw him staring down the panther as if it could see him. With a crash of its powerful jaws the panther jumped at Nick from the boulder.

Rolling aside he felt something at his waist snag on the rocky ground, the panther landing directly on top of him. It seemed to let out an almost human moan as Nick looked down with baited breath.

Jutted away from his body was the sword that had been sheathed at his waist, the blade pointing upwards. Leaning slightly to the side he could see the metal rising like a spire from the panthers back. It was only then that he became aware of the warm blood running down the sword and on to his shirt.

"The others will smell the blood," William whispered hurriedly. "We need to get out of here." Not waiting for a second invitation, Nick rolled the panther off him, pulling the sword from its lifeless body.

Following William around the boulder he adjusted the sheath back to its normal position. From the dead tree the bird watched them and when a fiery portal erupted in front of them neither gave it a second thought as they dived towards it.

Again the stench of sulphur that had encased them before pressed into Nick's lungs. This time it didn't linger, driven away by bright sunlight as they crashed on to a hard cobbled street. Around him there were shouts and screams too distorted by a spinning headache to make any sense of. Closing his eyes he allowed himself to fall into darkness, the sound of people running and shouting becoming more distant with every passing second. Wherever they had appeared now, he did not care. Anywhere was better than the hell they had just visited. With one last glimpse of the inside of his eyelids he passed out on the hard stone ground.

CHAPTER EIGHT
SECRETS OF A FATHER

There was something soft beneath him. A far contrast from the hard cobbles he had remembered from his last conscious moments. But this was not what had awoken him. The sound of someone banging on something had invaded his unconscious mind. Forcing his eyes open, he looked around.

He was back in his room, daylight flooding in through the small window opposite him. Squinting in the light he looked around for the source of the sound. With a hand raised to the glass was Rose, watching him from the other side of the window. Eyes blurry and the colours of the wooden walls distorted, he climbed out of bed, heading for the window.

"What's going on?" Nick asked as he flipped the catch, opening the window.

"I was just coming to see if you were alright," Rose replied.

"Couldn't it have waited until I had woken up?" he asked, annoyed that she had woken him for nothing.

"No, I was worried about you." When he rolled his eyes she continued quickly. "I found something as well, while you were away."

"But I was only gone for the night-" Nick began, breaking off when Rose shook her head vigorously.

"You were gone almost a week. No one knew where you had gone and then you appeared in the square, covered in blood." From her side she lifted a hand, passing a book through the window to him. "I found this in my father's things the other day."

"Why were you going through your father's things?" Nick asked as he took the battered, leather covered book.

"My mother has resigned herself to the fact that he is probably . . ." She replied, her voice fading away. Deciding not to ask, Nick let her trail off into silence.

The spine of the book was loose and cracked from use, the pages faded but the ink was still clear. On the pages there was line after line of neatly handwritten words in a midnight black ink.

"What am I looking for?" Nick asked as he thumbed through the pages until he reached the centre.

"Here," she said, pointing at the torn piece of paper lying in the centre of the book. The ink was faded. This page was clearly a lot older than any of the others. Looking down he began to read:

The . . . Prophecy of the . . . Phoenixes
The fires in The Temple of . . . once more as a search
for . . . a close.

Words from . . . lost to The . . . will aid . . . final search.

Ideas rushed around Nick's mind as he tried to replace the gaps that had been left by the faded words. Over and over he read the short passage and yet he was no closer to an answer.

"I thought it might help you," Rose said, watching as Nick read the passage again.

"One of the monks, Infinitas, told us that four parts of the prophecy were stolen years ago, two were lost in time and the only piece they had was the one we already knew," Nick muttered, more to himself than Rose. "Maybe this is one of the pieces that was stolen."

"I wonder who the book belonged to then," Rose said quietly.

"You said it was in your father's things."

"It was in his things but it can't be his. Most of it is in Latin and he never spoke any Latin."

"Who else could it belong to?" Nick asked, trying to think of anyone who had been close to Rose's father.

"It must have belonged to someone from the village because he never went to the cities from what I know," Rose said, voicing Nick's thoughts for him. For several minutes they both fell silent, neither sure of the next step they should take.

"I think the best thing to do would be to take it to William, if anyone knows enough Latin to translate it, it would be him," Nick said, handing the book back to Rose. When she nodded in silent agreement he continued. "I'll meet you in the square in a few minutes."

Ten minutes later and wrapped in a thick coat Nick entered the village square to find Rose leaning against the central stone. As he approached she looked up.

"Should we go?" Nick asked, nodding in the direction of the book that was tucked under her arm.

"I guess so," she sighed as she fell into step beside him. However, her tone was not lost on Nick.

"Is something wrong with that?"

"No," she replied, twiddling a piece of hair around her finger as she spoke.

"Now I know you're lying," he said with a quick glance across at her. When she looked at him in confusion he continued, a satisfied smirk crossing his lips. "When you lie you play with your hair."

Blushing slightly, knowing that he had got her beat, she dropped her hand to her side, walking on in silence for a few minutes.

"I just get the feeling there are things that William isn't telling me," she said quietly.

"Well I know I've told you everything that he told me," Nick replied defensively, not wanting to get involved in whatever was developing.

"Does it ever cross your mind that there might be more to this than he's telling us?"

"Do you trust me?" Nick asked, catching her off guard with the sudden change of subject. None the less, she nodded. "I trust that William has told us everything that is essential, if you don't trust him at least trust me."

"Okay, I trust you," she replied reluctantly as they turned the corner to face William's house.

Together they walked to the door, Nick raising a hand to knock loudly on the wooden panels. For a few seconds there was silence and then from somewhere inside there was the sound of someone shuffling around. From behind the door William revealed himself, eagerly waving them in from the cold.

Behind the enthusiastic facade, Nick could see something different in William. He looked tired with large bags under his eyes and he seemed unusually frail. His normally fluid movements were shaky and uncoordinated.

"Rose found this in her father's things, we were wondering if you would be able to take a look at it," Nick explained as he nudged Rose forward.

Pulling up a rickety looking wooden chair, William sat down behind the desk, looking across at Nick and Rose who stood before him. As she passed the book across the desk Nick could have sworn he had seen a shadow cross William's face.

"You said you found this in your father's things, do you ever remember seeing it before?" William asked quietly.

"I may have seen it once, when I was a lot younger," she replied after several minutes. "Do you know what it is?"

"It looks to be some form of diary," replied William. "Who the owner was is anybody's guess. As for what it is, it details an adventure, a search for objects that are thought to have mystical powers-"

"Could it be the stones?" Nick interrupted from the fringe of the conversation.

"From the diagrams and maps included amongst the diary entries, it would be reasonable for one to deduce that this is in fact the story of someone hunting the stones."

"But this doesn't make any sense." Rose contradicted. "Why would this be in my father's things? For one, he never spoke any Latin and two; he doesn't know anything about the stones other than what I told him."

"Maybe it was left to him by someone in the family," Nick said as he looked at the book. The cover definitely had the marks of something old.

"These are all possibilities, and though they are that they are still shots in the dark." William said, cutting across Rose as she opened her mouth to argue back. "We need to focus on the facts. An object of this nature is in our hands and not Numquam's. Without this he has no means of discovering the missing stones."

"How do we know he doesn't have other sources though?" Nick asked. "When I was in the forest that night looking for the lynx there were a group of people in grey cloaks in a small hollow. "What if he knows the other stones are here and he's sending out his followers to search around?"

Nick knew that he had stumbled on a worrying topic when William's face dropped, the bags under his eyes seemed to grow as the seconds of silence passed them by.

"What happened? Did you overhear anything?" William demanded. "Tell me everything you saw."

With that, Nick launched into his story about how he had tracked down the lynx and how, when it had awoken, it had chased him close to the clearing where he had seen the figures. For almost twenty minutes he continued to talk into the silence which was only broken by soft gasps from Rose whenever something remotely frightening happened.

" . . . that was when one of the cloaked figures killed the lynx. I decided to get out of there while I still could." Nick finished with a deep breath.

"This is a very concerning development. I fear we may be in a worse position than we originally believed," William muttered. "Thank you for telling me this."

"What should our next move be?" Rose asked quietly. "If he knows the stones are here then what's to stop him taking them and completing whatever ritual he needs to?"

"If, as Nick has told us, Numquam is already in possession of the death stone then the only thing that would prevent him would be the last stone," William whispered. "The Lava stone has been illusive for decades, without it the ritual cannot be completed."

"Do we go after the Lava stone if we find out where it is?" Nick asked, his mind working overtime to try and comprehend the trouble they would be in if they lost all of the stones. For several minutes they all fell into silence, each trying to develop a new plan.

"I think as soon as we discover the stones location we need to remove it, that way it will be under our protection," William said as he removed his glasses, cleaning them on his slightly grubby shirt. To this both Nick and Rose nodded in agreement.

"Would it be possible to replace the stone?" she asked. "You know, replace it with a fake stone-"

"And use that to throw off the ritual if Numquam does take the other stones," Nick cut in.

"That may just work," William muttered, more to the room in general than either of the two before him. "With some time I may be able to decipher some of the text in this book. That may give us a clue as to where to look for the stone. From there we will see what we can do."

With the promise that he would contact them when he was done, Nick and Rose left the house leaving William to set to work with the book.

CHAPTER NINE

PATH OF NIGHTMARES

Two weeks ago when Nick and Rose had left William with the book they had hoped for a quick solution followed immediately by action. There had been no such luck on either count. Each day, as the weather became more and more bitter there was still no progress.

It was the end of yet another disappointing and unyielding day as Nick downed the last of his warm raspberry juice before bed. Outside the warmth of the room sleet whirled around in the wind.

Nick felt as though he had barely drifted off to sleep when the door flew open with a bang. Shielding his eyes from the change in light, he looked towards the door. Between the wooden frames stood a figure huddled in a cloak. Struggling in the dark, he fought as he was pulled from the bed with surprising strength, yet he was not afraid. Surely this was just his mind creating a bizarre dream. Forced into the light he watched as the person lowered their hood to reveal a ghostly white face.

If he had not recognised William immediately he would have turned tail and run for his life. Before him the old man was physically shaking, his face drained of all colour. The dark bags that had become a permanent feature under his eyes stood out in stark contrast to the rest of his face. The eyes that were usually so calm had become stricken with fear as he looked around him.

"He knows!"

For several minutes they stood in silence, Nick trying to get his brain working after his sudden wake up while William's eyes continued to dart around the dark room.

"What's going on?" Nick asked, concerned. He had never seen anyone act this way before let alone William who was usually so calm.

"He knows that I know!" William repeated.

"Know what?" Nick asked, his mind still fuzzy and at a loss for what this conversation was about.

"The last stone. I was working at my desk when I finally managed to decipher the last part of the map-" William whispered desperately.

"But that's great! When do we leave?"

"I must have fallen asleep. The nightmare, it felt so real."

"What happened?" Nick asked, the enthusiasm dropping from his voice instantly like a rock in water.

"Come, I can't explain," William said, beckoning Nick towards the door. "I need to show you.

Having been dragged almost forcefully through the streets to William's house Nick sighed as he stood opposite the old man. Behind the desk he sat down, drawing a long slender pheasant's feather from a drawer. Muttering something inaudible under his breath he placed the tip of the feather to a yellowing piece of paper. In awe Nick watched as the feather began to move at speed although the owner of the hand that held it sat rigidly still with his eyes closed.

Looking at the scratches on the paper he watched as they began to fill with ink from no visible source. With one final scratch the feather stopped, falling silently to the desk. Eyebrows crinkled he looked up at William. His eyes were still closed. Whatever he was meant to see, it would be on the paper.

Disbelievingly he watched as the ink began to move on its own accord, winding and swirling over the paper until it began to form a picture.

He watched as in the centre the ink formed the shape of a cloaked figure, one that began to move forward between objects that took no real shape. For several seconds it moved until it came to a desk. Collapsed across the desk was an elderly man, a pen slipping from his hand over the desk covered in papers and books.

Although the figure in the drawing had no visible face Nick could feel it smiling as it reached out for what looked like a map. Carefully it examined the page with unseen eyes before pocketing it. Slowly the image began to change, the background reforming to make a statue of a phoenix. On a stone altar in front of the figure lay six objects, each as identically shaped as the other.

For a second time the picture reformed, showing a skeletal hand lifting as it made to remove the hood of the cloaked figure. With a bang the ink disappeared as William's hand hit the desk, his eyes shooting open.

"Did you see it?" William demanded desperately.

"Yes," Nick replied, slowly beginning to understand what he had seen. "The figure in the drawings, it was Numquam?"

To this William did not reply, merely nodded his head slowly.

"What does this mean?" Nick asked slowly.

"When I woke from the nightmare the door was just swinging closed, the paper I had been working on was gone." William muttered. "I am so sorry Nick."

"Sorry for what? You couldn't have done anything," Nick said, desperately trying to defend William as he berated himself.

"I believe the nightmare was real. It showed something of the past, present and future. The one from the present is obvious, as for the other two, it is anyone's guess." William confessed.

"But we know where the last stone is now," Nick said confidently. "All we need to do is get there before him and we can make the swap."

"If only it were so easy," William said with a shake of his head. "I believe I have completed the piece of the prophecy you showed me earlier." Looking down at the desk he began to read: "The fires in The Temple of Immortality will light once more as a search for eternal life comes to a close.

Words from a wise man lost to The Dark will aid evil's final search."

"William! No, we can't think like that," Nick argued. "Even if it is true we can still fight it. Like you said, part of the nightmare was from the future, we may be able to stop that happening."

"I'm sorry Nick. I betrayed you, just as he betrayed us," William conceded.

"You're not like him. You can put this right before he can do anything," Nick argued. "Don't you have something worth fighting for?"

For several minutes they fell into silence as William stared at the papers on the desk before him, a tear appearing in the corner of his eye. Trying to subtly wipe it away he looked back at Nick.

"You are right Nick. There is something worth fighting for. We need to do all we can to prevent this danger I have put everyone in," William whispered, his voice regaining some of its energy. "Where do we start?"

"The stone, where is it?" Nick questioned quickly.

"Here," William said as he pulled a map of an island between them. With one finger he pointed to a spot on the northern side of the island. "There is a unique canyon, shaped distinctly like a horseshoe. On the curved back wall there is a large waterfall behind which is a cave. From there it is unknown what we may face.

"How will we be getting there?"

"The usual transportation will suffice for this trip," William answered with a nod to a pile of stone tablets as Nick fired questions at him. "We will arrive on the central ridge of the horseshoe, from there we will need to walk."

"When do we leave?"

"As soon as you have everything you need, sword, staff and possibly the robe the monk's gave you for warmth. We will leave from the village square when you are ready."

With a nod Nick stood up, pushing himself away from the desk. There was no way William could have known what was going to happen. At least now they had the chance to put things right, Nick thought as he pocketed the replica of the stone they were about to try and take.

"Where is this place we are looking at by the way?" Nick asked, as the question jumped through the handful of others to the front of his mind.

"Iceland."

CHAPTER TEN
THE PEOPLE OF ASBYRGI

In an explosion of green sparks that broke the still morning air, Nick and William appeared. Before either of them could take in their surroundings they were thrust knee deep in snow. Regaining his balance, Nick blinked the falling snowflakes out of his eyes.

For almost as far as Nick could see, everything was covered in a thick untouched blanket of snow. Breaking the white on the horizon were steep grey cliffs, jagged even at this distance. It was only when the bitterly cold wind whipped around Nick's face that he looked down, finding himself inches from the edge of a cliff. Stepping back, Nick looked around properly for the first time since they had arrived.

Where he and William had arrived the ground was sloping downwards from the high ridge on which they stood. Around them, the valley curved, forming the horseshoe shape William had described back in Gladstow. Lining the valley floor were hundreds upon thousands of snow laden trees, bent double under the weight.

"That is where we are heading," William said, raising a hand, which shivered in the cold, to point to the far end of the valley. In the distance, Nick could make out something shimmering against the cliff face.

"What is this place?" shivered Nick as he and William began their descent into the snow carpeted valley.

"Welcome to Asbyrgi. This valley, although miles from any other civilisation, used to be home to a group of monks. From what little of their history we know, they took it upon themselves to protect the valley and ward off anyone who tried to get their hands on the stone hidden here. Anyone, except for The Saviour."

"It used to be home to them? Why did they leave?"

"You know the answer to that already, Nick," William replied. When Nick looked at him vaguely he began to elaborate. "When we visited the island of Akraneimacy, Infinitas told you the story-"

"Of how Senior Unus discovered the island after being forced from his home," Nick interrupted. "How does that fit into things though?"

"This is the place they were forced from years ago," William began. "At some point in time after his downfall, Numquam came back to this place. Whether he came looking for the stone or not, the monks never knew."

"They all ran when Numquam arrived?"

"Some of the monks escaped, yes."

"What happened to the others?" Nick asked as the track they had been making through the snow began to level out slightly, just above the tallest tree tops.

"Some of the monks stayed to fight, no one has heard anything from them since," William explained, pausing at the bottom of the slope to look around.

Cutting through the dense trees were two paths, one directly ahead of them, the other bearing slightly off to the right. After a moments thought, William led the way towards the path that continued straight ahead.

For the briefest moment as they passed between the trees, Nick saw something grey flicker through the trees. As they walked, the snow began to ease slightly. Face numb from the cold, he lowered his head momentarily to brush the flakes of snow from his eyes with a sleeve.

"It shouldn't be too much longer now," William said as the waterfall came into view through the trees for a second.

"You said you had all the stones at one time, do you remember what it was like in the caves?" asked Nick curiously.

"I must confess, Nick. I haven't ever been in any of the caves," William said, his voice dropping. "Your grandfather was the one who went after the stones. It was left to Numquam and myself to search for the clues, translate the Latin text and interpret the meaning of the prophecy."

"Did Numquam ever visit any of the caves?"

"He went along with your grandfather once," William replied. "That was when we were searching for the Earth stone. At the time neither of us could work out why he was so desperate to see what the caves were like."

"You know now though, don't you," Nick said. It was more of a statement than a question.

"Yes," William whispered gravely.

Before Nick could ask why, an arm was flung across his chest, stopping him dead in his tracks. Looking towards

William questioningly, Nick saw why he had stopped. Engrossed in their conversation they had wandered into a small clearing. That wasn't what had made William stop though and as Nick looked around he saw what had. Criss-crossing all over the clearing were tracks of footprints.

"I thought all of the people here disappeared," Nick said, turning on the spot. Leading out of the clearing were eight paths, all leading in different directions. Between the trees Nick saw movement. Behind him he heard a twig break.

"Stay exactly where you are!" a commanding voice bellowed from behind him before he could reach for the sword at his waist. "What are you doing here?"

"We were sent by the monks of Akraneimacy," William replied calmly.

"Why would they send you here? Those traitors!" spat the man.

"He's back." William said. "He will come for the stone sooner or later."

"It's been years since anyone has seen him. Even if he is back, we have guarded the stone for years."

"The Prophecy of the Phoenixes has begun, we have found The Saviour at last," William said, turning Nick to face the man he had been talking to.

Before him stood a man in a dusty grey cloak, the hood pulled over his head, casting his face into shadow. At his side he held a hooked pole, a lantern glowing a deep orange swinging slightly from it.

"Come," the man said as Nick felt his eyes settle on the phoenix that had been stitched into Nick's robe.

For what felt like the best part of an hour, Nick and William were escorted by the robed man. As the cliffs loomed over them an opening to a cave became visible, a light source flickering somewhere deep inside.

"This way please," the man gestured, allowing them to enter the cave first. Through the darkness, the outline of the rocks slowly began to emerge, the flickering light drawing closer with each passing second. Gently the cave broadened, expanding into a circular room. At its centre, a log fire crackled as it burnt in a small, stone enclosed pit.

Lingering in the shadows cast by the flames, several other cloaked figures were going about their own business. All of them wearing identical dusty grey cloaks with the hood pulled over their head. Moving towards the fire, Nick and William waited for the man who had accompanied them to join them.

When he emerged from the darkened tunnel, the man removed his hood. As the firelight flickered across his face it revealed thinning grey hair, pale wrinkled skin and slightly sunken blue eyes. Yet despite all the features that gave him age, he stood before them, smiling like a hopeful child.

"Please, have a seat," said the man. With a wave of his hand three wooden crates slid across the uneven floor to rest by the fire. For a moment he stood over Nick and William, watching them, before he sat opposite them. "Welcome to Asbyrgi. I am Brother Jameson. You say he has returned, how do you know it is him?"

"Since the ritual went wrong he has been trying to find me and retake the stones. Until a couple of months ago he had never been able to. One night he arrived in our village,"

William explained. "He tortured me for information on the stones. Since then, his bird has made several appearances in the woodland near the village, dropping a single feather on one occasion."

Withdrawing the feather from beneath his robe, William handed it to Brother Jameson, the firelight making the pure white of the feather sparkle momentarily. As he examined it Nick noticed some of the hooded figures breaking away from their own work to watch.

"You believe he is the one we have searched for?" Brother Jameson asked, using the feather to point in Nick's direction.

"On what grounds do you base your judgement, may I ask."

"When Nick's skin came into contact with one of the stones the stones moved. The five of the stones present began to orbit in perfect circles around an unseen object," William said quietly as more figures gathered around the fire. As Nick looked around the room Brother Jameson silently considered the new information.

"It would seem that you have come to a reasonable conclusion," Brother Jameson nodded, a smile breaking across his thin lips. "We have waited here, many days and nights for this moment to come. Forged from the stones of these sacred cliffs are one of our most highly guarded treasures, The Runes of Asbyrgi. They have protected us when the darkness threatened to overwhelm us so many years ago. You may have need for them in the future."

Before either Nick or William could say a word Brother Jameson rose from his makeshift chair, disappearing into the shadows of the room.

"What are The Runes of Asbyrgi?" Nick asked, his voice barely above a whisper, as he watched all the figures that had gathered around them by the fire.

"I believed them to be a legend," William replied. "Supposedly they would offer the wearer increased powers or powers they would normally be without." As Brother Jameson returned to the fireside they both fell silent again.

Swinging from the hand of Brother Jameson were two perfectly cut stone circles, smoothed down to form two discs. Through each one a hole had been made which held a strand of wool which had been tied to make a loop. As the firelight flickered across the stones, Nick saw a symbol etched in gold on each of the stones.

ᛝ ᚼ

"These are two of The Runes of Asbyrgi, the first for protection and the second for luck," Brother Jameson said as he passed them to Nick. "Take them and wear them well."

"Thank you," Nick said quietly as he hung each of them round his neck in turn, tucking them down the front of his robe. Against his skin he could feel the cold pressure of the stones.

"In this secluded place we don't often know what is happening in the outside world. If he truly has returned then we may need to consider action," said Brother Jameson loudly, drawing the rest of the cloaked figures into their conversation now. "Whatever lies in the outside world now, we do not know. Many great trials will lie ahead of you Nick. Always remember, no matter how dark it may seem you fight the good fight."

"Where you go from this place may not yet be known but you will be in all our thoughts and prayers. One day I hope we will meet once more on the battlefield that will rid this world of the evil that has attempted to consume it for the past forty years."

"Thank you," William said quietly as he shook hands with Brother Jameson. One by one the cloaked figures moved forwards, each taking it in turns to shake hands with William and Nick until finally Nick stood before Brother Jameson.

"In all my years I hoped I would one day get to meet The Saviour," whispered Brother Jameson. "The Phoenixes have blessed me with that gift. Now it all seems so unfair that such a heavy weight should rest on the shoulders of someone as young as yourself. I have seen your dream, I know you have spoken with one of The Phoenixes."

"How did you know that?" Nick asked, almost stunned into silence by the revelation the old man was making.

"Maybe it is the magic imbedded in this place that has give us the powers we have now. Maybe it is not," Brother Jameson said. "Whether it is one or the other, it does not matter. What matters now is The Saviour has been found. Now we can end what started so many years ago. Travel safely young Nick."

"Are you going to accompany us to the cave?" Nick asked as he shook hands with Brother Jameson.

"I'm afraid not. A very select few are allowed to enter The Sanctuary. I am not one of those," explained Brother Jameson. "When you leave this cave you will see three paths, take the right-hand path. That will lead you along the cliff face to the cave entrance. Perhaps you will see The Oracle on the way there."

"Who is The Oracle?" asked Nick curiously.

"The Oracle is our leader," said Brother Jameson. "Every day for as long as any of us can remember he has spoken of The Saviour, of how the time he will join us is drawing closer. I find it curious that the one day he doesn't speak of The Saviour you arrive."

"Where did he go if he knew today would be the day I would come here?" a perplexed Nick asked.

"Many of us believed he would only say it each day to keep everyone's hopes up, that today might finally be the day," whispered Brother Jameson. "However this morning he spoke no words to any of us. He left the cave in the direction of The Sanctuary and hasn't returned since."

"Which way do we go once we get to The Sanctuary?" William asked from behind Nick.

"If you follow the cliff face round you shouldn't be able to go far wrong with finding the waterfall," Brother Jameson said. "From what The Oracle has revealed to us about the inside of The Sanctuary, the entrance to the cave is somewhere behind the waterfall."

Thanking Brother Jameson for all his help, Nick and William headed for the tunnel that would take them back outside. Bidding everyone a final goodbye they left behind the warmth of the fire-lit room for the dark tunnel.

CHAPTER ELEVEN
THE CAVE OF THE GUARDIAN

Following the instructions of Brother Jameson, Nick and William exited the cave and began along the right-hand path of the three. True to his word, it followed along the base of the cliffs. Ahead of them a single track of footprints, which Nick believed to be The Oracle's, led the way through the snow.

In the distance the ever increasing sound of water crashing against rocks told them they were heading in the right direction.

"Do you think The Oracle knew we would be coming today?" asked Nick in an attempt to break the silence that had fallen between him and William since they had left the cave.

"I don't know, it does seem odd that he would break with tradition after so long though," William replied. Ahead of them the path began to rise steeply along the cliff face. Climbing higher, the snow on the path seem to grow shallower as though there was something below the surface melting it away.

The ledge they walked along slowly rose above the tops of the spindly, snow laden trees. As it reached its peak the slope flattened out, forming a narrow path that hugged the cliff face. The first thing that caught Nick's eye was the emerald green lake far below them, set amongst the snowy trees like a gem. From the cliffs high above the lake water tumbled over the edge, sparkling as it fell.

Awestruck by the view, the man who sat cross legged at the edge of the path looking out over the lake went unnoticed by Nick until his weak cough broke the silence.

"Welcome to Asbyrgi, Nick Harrison," whispered the man. "I have waited many years for your arrival."

"You are The Oracle?" Nick asked, cautiously moving forwards.

"Yes."

"Brother Jameson said you would be out here," William said, moving so he stood beside Nick.

"I am glad Brother Jameson found you. Tell me, did he take you to the cave?"

"He gave me these," Nick replied, digging the runes, that Brother Jameson had given him, from beneath his robe.

"Ah, The Runes of Asbyrgi," The Oracle said quietly as he turned one of them between his fingers. "These two have been kept by our people for generations, waiting for the time when The Saviour would come to us."

"Brother Jameson sent us in this direction, he said the entrance to the cave was hidden behind the waterfall somewhere," Nick said, returning the runes, that The Oracle had now released, to the inside of his robe.

"In all the years I have spent here, guarding The Sanctuary from all evil," The Oracle began, "I have never seen the entrance to the cave which you seek. Many times in my younger years I ventured behind the waterfall but all I ever saw were runes carved into the stone."

"What do the runes say?" Nick asked, eyeing the waterfall behind The Oracle.

"There are two lines of text, the first reads: The Saviour must take a leap of faith." The Oracle breathed. "As for the second line, when it became clear the text was not intended for anyone but myself, I did not go as far as to translate it."

Sparing the waterfall a glance, The Oracle reached within the cloak he wore to reveal a small book. After briefly checking the first few pages he handed it to Nick.

"This will give you all the information that you need to decipher the runes and any others you may find on your journey," The Oracle explained. "May your journey be safe and the trials you will face be overcome."

"Thank you," Nick said quietly as he tucked the book inside his robe.

"I must leave you now and return to my people," The Oracle said as he rose to his feet. As he began to walk down the slope, away from Nick and William it became apparent how frail the old man was. When The Oracle had disappeared from view amongst the snowy trees, William turned to Nick and with a nod they began to descend the ledge towards the lake.

It was a torturous twenty minutes before Nick and William stood on the edge of the lake; its green waters sparkling like millions of tiny emeralds. Finding a way through the dense trees had proved more difficult than first thought, all the while the waterfall lay just out of their reach, teasing them it seemed.

Cautiously they made their way along the bank of the lake, William leading the way. Looking out across the lake it was several moments before Nick realised what was wrong with the image he was seeing. For all the water that came tumbling over the cliff high above them not a single ripple was being created in the lake. To Nick, it seemed as if the lake didn't exist in respect to the waterfall and yet as he crouched down beside it he could feel the water with his fingertips.

"Come Nick, I think it is best that we don't delay any longer," William said quietly when he realised Nick had stopped following him.

"Look at the waterfall," Nick pointed out. "It's as if the water is passing through the surface of the lake."

"Brother Jameson did say that there was magic embedded in this place," William reminded Nick as he set off around the lake again.

As they drew up next to the waterfall the sound of the tumbling water became deafening, leading Nick to shout to William as he spotted a narrow pathway, barely wide enough for him to walk along. Withdrawing the book of runes that The Oracle had given him he looked back to William who stood beside the lake.

"The Oracle said the runes were somewhere behind the waterfall," Nick called to William as he began to edge his way along the path. Ahead of him he could see the gold of the runes shining on the cliff face. As he got closer he examined them.

⚹ ⱶⱯ V̈ Ҷ Ⱥ F Oɣ Ħ

Ж ɰ ⊙ ⚹ Ю Oɣ ⚹ ⱶⱯ

    Slowly, one by one, Nick began to decipher the runes. Taking the small pencil that had been left inside the cover he noted down each rune, marking the meaning of each one beside it. It was a long and arduous job, progress was slow but finally Nick edged his way back along the path towards William who stood waiting patiently.

"Did you manage to decipher the runes?" asked William.

"Eventually," Nick replied as he looked down at the notes he had made. "It reads: The Saviour must take a leap of faith. Echoes will light the path of The Saviour."

"Could you see the entrance to the cave while you were working on the runes?" William asked as he looked at the translation Nick had made.

"There wasn't anything there except the runes. It was just a straight cliff face," Nick replied, looking back over his shoulder at the waterfall.

"A leap of faith . . ." William muttered to himself. Taking in their surroundings once more he could still see nothing but the snowy mass of trees and the emerald lake.

"Do you think it could be under the surface of the lake?" Nick asked as he watched where the waterfall was hitting the surface without leaving a trace. "What if the surface is just an image meant to hide the entrance?"

"It is a possibility, yet the surface still bears the resemblance and properties consistent with water," William noted, as he used his free hand to test the water.

"Surely it's worth a try though," Nick said. "We've come too far to give up and leave with nothing.

"Very well, Nick," William said resignedly. Muttering something inaudible as he passed a hand over the book of runes, he handed it back to Nick. "You had best take this with you. If you do find the entrance to the cave there is no telling what you will find inside. It may be useful to you in some way."

"What are you going to do?" Nick asked curiously as he tucked the book inside his robe.

"I will return to The People of Asbyrgi," William began. "If you have not returned in two hours I will come after you."

With a nod, Nick acknowledged William's plan. Leaving with a wave and a wish of good luck the old man turned, heading back into the snowy forest. All alone by the side of the lake Nick took a moment to marvel at the place he stood in. Never had he seen somewhere more perfect. Without the rumbling of the waterfall it would have been perfectly silent.

Shaking the thoughts from his mind, he turned to the lake. With the cold stone runes pressing against the skin on his chest and the book weighing down the inside pocket of his robe, he dived.

Pain, like a thousand shards of glass slashed at his skin. The ice cold water blistered at his face as he kicked his way to the surface again.

As the top of his head broke the surface he opened his eyes. Carefully treading water he looked around him, trying to gather his bearings. Behind him the sound of the waterfall filled his ears. During his dive he had ended up somewhere towards the middle of the lake. Knowing he wouldn't be able to stay above the surface much longer without the icy water cramping his muscles he turned to face the waterfall, diving again.

Opening his eyes underwater, the emerald colour that had tainted the surface seemed to have disappeared, the water now a clear, sparkling blue. Kicking forwards, Nick swam towards the waterfall that plunged through the water. Slowly he began to feel his lungs tightening as his supply of oxygen began to dwindle. Before he could begin to kick for the surface once more he felt something take hold of his ankle, pulling him down into the depths of the lake.

Panic stricken, he kicked wildly, trying to free himself. Twisting and turning, Nick looked down at his ankles to find nothing there but the depths of the lake, still with no sign of the bottom. Above him the little daylight that had found its way to Asbyrgi had disappeared. He was lost, disorientated in the growing darkness as some unknown force pulled him down into what he was sure would now be his watery grave.

When he could hold his breath no longer Nick opened his mouth, waiting for the rush of icy water to fill his lungs. But none came. Instead all he felt was air. What magic had been placed on this lake, he didn't care right now. The moment when he had thought all was lost, he had been saved. With renewed faith he twisted and turned, searching for the waterfall, the one thing that would give him the bearing he needed.

Out of the darkness it appeared, sparkling just as it had been when he had stood beside William on the edge of the lake examining it. Moving towards it he dived again, forcing himself further into the darkness.

Suddenly the waterfall disappeared from beside him, his guide had vanished. Moving towards where it should have been he saw a sight that made his heart leap. A rock face, unlike the one above the surface, an area of darkness sat in the centre. An entrance. The entrance he had been searching for.

Ignoring the screams of his muscles, Nick started forwards, swimming desperately for the opening in the rock. This is it, he thought as he got closer, finally. Using his hands to help guide him, Nick pulled himself into the cave. The dark rock was sharp and jagged against his skin, more than once he felt it break through. He was certain that when he found his way to the surface there would be cuts and bruises all over his hands and arms. Somehow it didn't seem to concern him.

Almost at the point of exhaustion he saw it. A light. Somewhere up ahead there was a way out of the freezing water.

With one final kick Nick broke through the surface. Releasing a desperate gasp for air that he only just realised he had been holding back, he swam towards the rocky ledge on the far side of the cavern. Soaking and chilled to the bone he pulled himself up on the rock, hoisting himself from the water. Leaning back against the wall he closed his eyes, taking in as much of the air as he could with each breath.

Slowly he felt his muscles beginning to relax, the pain subsiding. Opening his eyes he looked around, taking in his new surroundings properly for the first time. To his left a flickering green glow led the way into another tunnel, the one, he was sure, that would take him to the Lava stone. By the entrance a single torch sat, cradled in a metal bracket that had been fixed to the wall. Like all the other light in the cave it was green.

Standing up, Nick removed it from its holder in order to explore more of the room he had arrived in. All he could make out besides the large pool were stone paths on three of the sides. It must be some kind of receiving chamber, he thought as he examined the walls. At his eye level was a single band of golden runes that seemed to run continuously repeating themselves around the room.

Ѭ Ж O Ẕ Ш Д W̄ ђ ∴

Remembering William's warning that they should not delay any longer than necessary, he merely jotted the symbols in the front of the book The Oracle had given him. True to his promise, William's magic had kept the book dry.

Returning the book to the inside pocket of his robe, Nick looked towards the tunnel that led out of the chamber. Wishing that he could have stayed as dry as the book, he moved forwards. Pushing his dripping hair from his eyes he saw the runes continuing into the tunnel, as if they were leading him forwards. Of all the runes he had seen on the wall he only recognised two of them, the ones that resembled 'Saviour' and 'Echoes'.

Beneath the sleeves of his robe Nick felt the hairs on the backs of his arms stand up, tingling with the feel of magic. As soon as he stepped into the tunnel he realised what the magic was.

From nowhere a wave of heat blasted over him, driving out the bitter coldness that had reached his bones and replacing it with a gentle warmth. The robe that had been heavy with water and leaving a dripping trail behind him was dry once more.

The further Nick walked into the tunnel the brighter the light seemed to grow, almost as if it was drawing power from what lay deep inside the ancient cave. Taking a sharp turn to the right the tunnel suddenly disappeared, laying bare one of its magnificent secrets.

Glowing off the steep rock faces was the light of hundreds of green torches, each one burning merrily in its holder. Winding its way through the centre of the cavernous room was a steep staircase, lit on either side by the green flames that adorned the cave.

Awestruck, Nick began to move forwards towards the staircase. Through the semi-darkness he could see a beacon of light, high above where he stood now at the end of the stone stairs. The only thing standing between him and the other side were the ancient steps. It wasn't until Nick reached the edge that he realised there was nothing surrounding the staircase except darkness, nothing except a fall into the chasm below.

Curiously, Nick took a stone that lay on the ground close by. Dropping it over the edge he waited, counting silently in his head as he waited for the sound of the stone hitting the bottom.

For a full ten seconds there was silence, until finally, somewhere far below he heard the clink of the stone striking a hard surface far below. Putting the thought of the deadly drop out of his mind, he took the first step.

His foot had barely come into contact with the thin layer of dust on the step when all of the torches went out, all except the one he was carrying.

"Great," Nick muttered to himself, his voice echoing around the now almost pitch-black cavern.

Chapter Twelve
THE STAIRCASE OF ECHOES

The light from the torch that Nick carried, which was now the only source in the cavern, barely stretched more than a couple of feet ahead of him. Deciding to take it one step at a time he began his climb, slowly making his way towards the faint light some hundred feet above where he now stood. Using it as a marker for where he needed to go he tried to visualise the staircase he had seen before the lights went out.

It was barely a dozen steps up that he heard something, the sound of movement. Careful to keep his balance, Nick looked over one shoulder. There was nothing there. Dismissing it as a trick of his mind, he continued.

Several steps later he could no longer put it down to his imagination. This time he was sure he heard a shout, a shout of a man, someone who stood somewhere out of sight, enveloped in the darkness. Desperate to prove the part of him that thought it was a trick wrong, Nick turned, sitting down on the step behind him. In silence he waited, his eyes raking through the darkness in search of the owner of the voice.

"This way," shouted the voice. It was closer this time. In the direction that Nick knew the tunnel lay something appeared. Whatever it was, it had a faint blue glow to it. Was it a phoenix like the one he had seen in the tunnels beneath Gladstow? Thinking back on it now, it almost seemed like a lifetime ago.

Slowly the figure began to move forwards. That was when Nick noticed the torch in its hand. Unlike his, it no longer burnt green but a pale blue like the figure. As it drew closer Nick picked up on the sound of a voice.

"We need to move quickly, The People of Asbyrgi will come looking for us soon," spoke the figure.

The figure appeared to be speaking to someone that Nick couldn't see. Cautiously Nick stood up, moving towards the figure.

"Hello?" Nick called, his voice echoing around the cavern. For a moment it looked as if the figure was about to respond until it stepped on to the first step and froze.

"I don't know, I just stepped on the first step and the lights went out," said the figure, looking sideways to its invisible companion. After a pause it continued. "No, I don't think even William would be able to work this one out."

Shock. It was the only way to describe what Nick now felt. Like a ton of bricks crashing down on him he realised who he must be seeing. Forty years after his disappearance Nick's grandfather had returned, unknowing of the son who had been born nine months after his disappearance and the existence of his grandson who now stood before him, walking the same path that he had once walked.

Slowly Nick realised who the ghostly figure must be talking to. Invisible to him, Nick knew that forty years ago Numquam himself had stood here. Had he already been plotting to take the stones for himself? Did he know he would shortly betray his friends in the hope of personal gain?

As he watched the figure begin to climb the steps, passing straight through him, Nick thought back to all the runes. Now he understood. 'Echoes will light the path of The Saviour.' The ghostly echo of his grandfather was here to lead him through this maze of darkness. From beyond the grave he was still there, helping Nick.

Turning, Nick began to climb the staircase again, following in the ghostly footsteps of his grandfather. In the wake of the ghostly figure echoes of one half of a conversation drifted back to Nick.

It was twenty minutes of climbing later, as Nick neared a platform on the staircase that the figure disappeared. With caution, he approached it, still fighting not to look down into the darkness of the chasm below him.

Stepping on to the platform, Nick looked around. Judging by the faint glow of light, from the room that he knew to be at the top of the stairs, he must be about halfway. If not for the faint hissing sound it could have been several moments longer before Nick looked down.

Around the edges of the platform he could make out faint wisps of what looked like smoke. Turning on the spot he saw it emerging from all sides of the stone square that he stood on. As the smoke thickened he noticed that it was beginning to take a faint blue colour.

Unnerved, firstly by the sudden disappearance of his ghostly guide and now the smoke that appeared without a visible source, Nick moved for the staircase that would take him away from the platform and higher above the chasm. But his escape route was met with resistance, an invisible force pushing him back.

Stumbling as he tried to regain his balance, Nick turned frantically on the spot, searching for the other staircase, the one that would take him back towards the exit of the cave. Slowly the blue mist was rising; engulfing all of his surroundings and hiding form view his only other chance at an escape route.

As he stood there the mist continued to rise. Waist height, chest height, head height, until it towered over him, trapping him inside some kind of box.

Trying to keep level-headed, Nick moved towards the mist. If he could find out what he was up against then he may be able to find a way to counter it. But no matter which way he moved he couldn't get within a foot of the blue screen. After several attempts to reach out at it with his hand, all unsuccessful, he gave up.

Beginning to feel slightly claustrophobic, Nick looked around him. The mist, whatever it was, was on the move again. No longer growing higher it seemed to be closing in on him, slowly squeezing all of the breathable air from the area. Disorientated and with a lack of landmarks for reference he turned blindly, panicking as the space he stood in grew ever smaller. Beneath his rib cage he felt his lungs tighten, exhausting the little oxygen they had left, until pinpricks of black began to fill his vision, his head spinning.

Through the darkness that was prickling his vision he saw a flash of gold on the floor. Another rune.

ρ

Consciousness began to drift away from Nick as he felt himself falling. In the distance he heard a clang of metal as the sword at his waist struck the stone, his hands stretching out in front of him to break his fall. He felt the uneven rock against his skin, piercing it, small beads of blood leaking from the cuts on to the platform. And then, for a single moment, there was nothing. Perfect silence. Perfect darkness. From some unknown direction the ghostly words of his grandfather echoed as Nick slipped into the darkness.

"It wants blood."

From somewhere in the distance there was light, light of a green colour. Confused, Nick watched as it grew closer, flickering slightly around the insides of his eyelids. For what could have been minutes or perhaps hours he watched it draw nearer before he became aware of his other senses.

Somewhere around waist height he could feel the cold metal of the sword pressing gently against his skin. Across his chest and one side of his face the cold metal was replaced with cold, uneven rock. The smell of wet rock and dust clung to the insides of his nostrils and as he opened his eyes a sliver he sneezed.

For several moments he sat quite still, taking in all around him. He was in the centre of the stone platform that formed the halfway point of the staircase he had been climbing earlier. The blue mist that had surrounded him, almost suffocating him, had vanished without a trace. In its wake it had left the torches that surrounded the cavern burning again. Their green light bouncing off the sheer rock faces. Several feet to his right his own torch lay extinct. Pulling it towards him, he looked around for somewhere to reignite it.

Unsteadily Nick clambered to his feet. As he pushed himself up he felt the sting of the rock against a cut. Looking down he saw a single cut on his right hand, one that perfectly mirrored the one that had been there months ago when Rose had pulled the sword from his hand in Gladstow. It was as if the cut had never left his palm and just been reopened by his fall.

Looking around at the floor for what could have caused it he saw nothing. The rock was uneven but there was nothing sharp enough to carve that kind of cut in his skin. All that proved what had happened there was the small gathering of blood drops around the rune on the floor which now burnt a fierce gold. Brighter by far than any of the others he had ever seen.

"Come, it is this way," whispered the ghostly voice of Nick's grandfather from behind him. Turning, he saw him. Standing at the base of the ascending staircase was the pale figure, staring at the exact spot where Nick stood now. As if, at last he could see Nick.

Without another word he moved away, taking the steps slowly as he glanced back over his shoulder, like he was waiting for Nick to follow. Hesitating slightly, Nick followed, hurrying so that he could walk beside the man he had never known in life.

"You have done well," he said gently, sparing a glance in Nick's direction. Yet Nick knew in his heart, this man wasn't talking to him but the man who would soon betray him. "It is so close now. Can you feel it?"

With a rush Nick felt it, as if the whispered words had opened the flood gates to all sorts of feeling. When he had entered the cave with Brother Jameson he had felt the magic tingle across his skin, likewise when he had stood beside the lake with William. But this was different. This was stronger, far stronger than any magic he had ever felt. Like a waterfall breaking over his head, soaking him to every nerve ending. This was power beyond anything and he could feel it to his very core.

Beneath his feet the steps were becoming rougher and steeper with each passing minute. It was as if the lower steps had been worn down by people seeking the stone and none had made it this far, none as far as he knew except his grandfather and Numquam. Now he was following in their footsteps.

But his goal was different from both of theirs. He was not here to take the stone for his own gain; he was here to protect it, to stop it falling into the wrong hands. This was the thought that drove him on, past the aches and pains in his tired legs and the exhaustion that was threatening to overtake him at any moment.

As the staircase neared its destination it began to change direction viciously, first jutting to the left and then doubling back on itself. The golden light that poured from the room high above the chasm seemed to pulse.

For all the way he had come it was only now that Nick felt a twinge of fear somewhere inside his gut. Nerves were beginning to pick holes in him. What would he find at the top of the stairs? Would the stone be there? Would there be something there that would try and kill him for a third time like the lake and the mist had already attempted to?

Unsettled by his thoughts, Nick hurried on, overtaking the figure of his grandfather now. Forcing himself to try and think of other things he scrambled up the steps, slipping and sliding and so many times, nearly falling towards the chasm of darkness beneath him.

Ahead of him he could see the steps running out, the golden light calling him, urging him on and driving him closer to what he was seeking.

Unnoticed and far behind Nick the ghostly figure stopped on the steps. This time it was watching the living, breathing person ahead of him, not the invisible form of his friend that was trapped in the past with him. With a relieved sigh and an unspoken wish of luck the figure faded away, returning to the darkness of the cavern.

With the figure fading behind him, Nick scrambled over the last few steps, collapsing on to the stone ledge, basking for a moment in the golden light that flooded over him. Closing his eyes he allowed himself to release the breath he didn't realise he had been holding. All he had to do was find the stone, get out of the cavern with it and it would all be over. He had lost track of time inside the cave, would William be waiting for him with The People of Asbyrgi? Was he already on his way to find Nick?

Slowly Nick took to his feet once more, examining his surroundings where the green light from the staircase collided with the golden light from the next chamber.

Along the edge of the platform, that seemed to stretch the width of the cavern, green torches stood atop pillars carved of stone every few feet. Between them they marked the edge of the stone ledge and the plummet of who knew how far into the darkness of the chasm.

Turning, Nick looked towards the golden light. It was distant but at the same time so bright, almost blinding. Before him the cliff face formed a narrow archway, the entrance to the room blocked by a heavy metal gate. For a long way, what could be hundreds of feet, there was nothing but darkness. The golden light Nick had seen was a thin, narrow beam falling from high in the room on to a plinth that he knew must hold the stone.

How strange it was that a light so bright didn't illuminate anything inside the room other than the stone, Nick thought as he looked between the metal rails. The stone seemed to be calling to him, whispering in a disembodied voice inside his head.

"Come for me. Take me. Think of the power you could have. With the stones he would be no match for you. You could rule the world. All would cower before you, be at your mercy."

Inside his head the words reverberated, echoing over and over. Everything around him seemed to vanish as he stood transfixed, staring at the stone that seemed to sparkle. The longer he looked at it the stronger its pull became.

Moving without instruction his legs began to carry him forwards, towards the metal gate. The harder Nick tried to force himself to look away the harder the stone pulled, drawing him closer until his nose was barely an inch from the cold metal.

From his sides, Nick felt his arms lifting, his hands pushing towards the twisted metal. He felt the icy coldness of the gate at his fingertips before he came into contact with it. But when his hands touched it he didn't feel cold. All he felt was pain, the metal burning against his palms, stabbing into the open cut across his hand. With a scream that echoed around the cavern, Nick yanked his hands away from the gate.

With a resonating crash it flew open, bouncing off the rock face it was fixed to. Pulling back Nick stumbled, falling to the ground, finally breaking his gaze with the stone that had held him captivated.

Looking down at his hands he saw the pattern of the metal burnt into the skin on his palms. On his right hand the cut from his earlier fall was bleeding again. Dabbing at it with his robe, Nick pulled himself to his feet again, glancing in the direction of the stone that still sat on its plinth. This time nothing happened. There was no voice in his head. No pull from an invisible force.

Slowly and cautiously, Nick made his way towards the stone arch. Pushing the gate back gently he winced, expecting it to burn his skin again. But it didn't, it just swung back against the rock. Taking a deep breath Nick stepped over the threshold, determined to finish this as quickly as possible now.

CHAPTER THIRTEEN
BEFORE THE ALTAR

In the distance, close to the plinth where the stone sat, the ghostly figure appeared again. Silently Nick watched from the gateway as he picked up an imitation of the stone, stowing it away safely in his cloak. Slowly, Nick moved forward.

Flames burst into life on either side of him as he moved forward. The stone dishes that contained the flames sat at the base of towering statues.

On each side of the path sat three identical statues, all of a phoenix perched on a stone wall that rose from the water that flowed on either side of the path. Behind the plinth at the far end of the room he could see a seventh statue. This one, however, had its wings spread, as if it had been captured in stone as it was about to take off.

Spending several awestruck moments marvelling at the detail in the carvings, Nick wondered who had created them. How long had they been here?

Nick's footsteps echoed around the cave as he moved forward, across the stone floor. Passing each set of opposing statues, flames burst into life beneath them, filling them with a dull flickering glow.

Gently the path began to widen, spreading into a large circular area in the centre of the room. Around the edges water stretched into the darkness as far as he could see. In the distance he could hear it lapping at what he guessed to be the rock walls.

In the centre of the stone circle sat the plinth with the Lava stone resting on it. Set behind it was the statue of the phoenix with its wings spread. Compared to the other statues he had walked past, it must have been about twice the size. With a half-light surrounding him, Nick noticed the beauty of the place. Yet, if no one was supposed to find the stone why bother? What was the point in the hundreds of hours it must have taken to carve each statue if no one was meant to see them?

Drawing the replica of the Lava stone from inside his robe, Nick placed it on the plinth. William's recreation of the stone was perfect, an identical shape and size. Even the darker spots in the garnet were exact. In the bright light that filtered down from above they sparkled like identical twins.

Carefully Nick reached forwards, gripping the real stone in his hand; he lifted it from its resting place. Beneath the stone he felt the skin on his hand grow warm. Passing the stone to his left hand, he examined his right. The burns he had received from the gate were fading until only the diagonal cut across his palm remained. Absorbed in the magic the stone was producing Nick didn't notice as the flames that lit the pathway between the statues flickered out, one by one, until only the light that fell on his shoulders was left.

Pocketing the stone, Nick looked at the fake stone on the plinth. It was only then, carved in gold on the plinth, that four runes caught his eye.

Ⱏ Д Щ Ѣ

Taking the book of runes from inside his robe, Nick began to flick through the pages, oblivious of the darkness behind him.

"The ghosts will return," Nick whispered after several minutes, having found what he was looking for in the book. As the words left his lips there was a crash somewhere far behind him.

Turning round slowly, Nick looked in the direction of where the gate had been, now obscured by the darkness. In the distance he could make out a faint blue light that had replaced the green that lined the staircase. With every passing second it seemed to pulse as it grew brighter.

For seconds that stretched slowly to minutes, Nick stood transfixed, watching, waiting for the source of the light to show itself.

With one final pulse it appeared in the gateway, illuminating the iron work that was still open against the rock. For a moment it hovered, completely still, before moving towards Nick. As it drew closer it came into focus. The pulsing Nick had seen was in time with each beat of the bird's wings and, as it settled on the plinth, he recognised it as a phoenix.

"You are the phoenix, aren't you?" Nick asked quietly.

"The ghost of one, but yes, essentially that is correct," replied a bodiless voice, while the phoenix shifted its feet lightly.

"You're the one that I saw back in Gladstow," Nick said as he took a step towards the bird which eyed him cautiously.

"No. I do not believe we have ever met, Nick Harrison," replied the voice. "Look closer, at my feathers. Are they the same as the ones of the phoenix you saw several months ago?"

Unfurling its wings the phoenix relaxed, allowing Nick to approach it. At the very tips of its wings the blue feathers turned a bright orange, identical to that of the replica stone that sat on the plinth beside it.

"Not the same phoenix as you saw before, am I?"

"Sorry," Nick apologised quickly.

Cocking its head to one side, the phoenix examined Nick. Or that was how he thought of it. Was it judging him? Deciding whether or not he was worthy of more of the secrets that it possessed?

"What are you doing here?" asked Nick slowly. "How are you here?"

"I am here in the same manner as the other ghost you passed earlier. A mere imprint of a moment lost in the weaving fabric of time," replied the phoenix. "As for why I am here, I come bearing a warning, a warning that was written for you, hidden away in a prophecy a thousand years ago. My piece, amongst the many that led to the creation of the legend that you see."

"Your piece?"

"Surely you didn't think that there being seven prophecies and seven phoenixes was a coincidence," said the phoenix. Before Nick the bird seemed to hang its head as if in disappointment.

"Sorry," Nick apologised again.

Suddenly before his eyes, the phoenix grew rigid, its wings spread as it stared at Nick. At the first eye contact it began to speak, this time the voice was a different one however, one that echoed around the dark room.

"The fires in the Temple of Immortality will burn once more as a search for understanding comes to a close."

"Words from a man lost to the Stones of Immortality will aid The Saviour's final search."

As the phoenix finished its speech its body relaxed again, its wings tucking back in again. For several seconds it sat still, blinking at Nick as he watched it curiously.

"The Temple of Immortality?" Nick asked.

"A most sacred place. The place where all of the stones will be united, granting the power of immortality to the holder," explained the phoenix.

"I read somewhere that once all of the phoenixes were dead the power of the stones would break," Nick said. "Does that mean that at least one of the other phoenixes is still alive?"

"Although none of the phoenixes are still alive not all of them are dead," said the phoenix quietly. "While the ghost of one of the phoenixes remains in the world of the living they are not truly dead. Therefore the power still remains. However, it is weakened somewhat by the lack of a physical link in your world."

"The piece I read also spoke of the dying embers of a phoenix and a sword created from them. What does that mean if all of the phoenixes are already ghosts?"

"When I say that all of the phoenixes are dead, I mean the ones that helped to create the seven stones," said the phoenix. "One phoenix, however, remains in the world of the living although none of my brothers would recognise it as one of their own. The sword of which you speak is believed to exist. Where it is hidden, I could not tell you though."

"At the time of the creation of the stones they were created to guard the immortality of the phoenixes. It wasn't until several years later that it was realised what had been created. It was a . . . misjudgement on our part. You see, by binding one piece of a phoenixes soul to an object that remains in the world of the living it could not fully die. What went unrealised is how powerful those objects became."

"Realising what had been created, we took it as our duty to guard the stones, protecting them from falling into the hands of mortals. For centuries the stones remained safe, unknown to the rest of the world, protected by all kinds of magical tests and tricks. That was when the prophecies came."

"One long winter night a thousand years ago there were dreams, nightmares that showed a dark future. Slowly they were compiled, taking the shape of the seven prophecies that exist today. Through time their only trace was lost though, or that was what the belief was until The Adventurer came in search of the stones. Slowly, one by one the stones disappeared along with the phoenix that guarded it."

"You said there was another phoenix though," Nick interrupted.

"The eighth phoenix disappeared as well. It left behind no trace except an empty cave where it had hidden one part of its own soul. For a long time it was presumed the stone was stolen like the others, that was when they came here. They came with the other stones, it was not with them, I could not sense its power," the phoenix continued. "When it became apparent that the phoenix had taken its stone when it disappeared, the others stopped recognising it as one of their own."

"What became of the stone is anyone's guess. We were only left with the information that a safety net was to be put in place in case the other stones fell into the wrong hands."

"What do you believe happened to the stone?" Nick asked, drawn deeper into the story in search of information about what his grandfather may have been doing.

"I believe the stone is still out there, where though I don't know," replied the phoenix. Before the phoenix continued there was an echoing crash from somewhere in the direction of the staircase. A glow of green light had returned, flooding into the altar room. "I fear our time here is up now Nick Harrison. It would be best for you to flee I believe."

"It's alright. It's probably just William coming looking for me," Nick reassured the phoenix as it began to hop towards the edge of the pedestal.

"It is not the one you wish to see," said the phoenix. "I must leave you now."

"Wait!" Nick called after the bird as it took flight, heading for the exit of the altar room. "Where is he? Where is his body? Please, I want to find him."

"His body rests in the place where it fell," echoed the voice of the phoenix. "He rests in the Temple of Immortality."

With a deafening crack that resonated through the cave the phoenix disappeared, leaving Nick alone in the semi-darkness. Looking around, he tried to find another route out of the cave, somewhere to hide, anything to help him escape from what he knew was coming.

Numquam was here. He was coming for the stone and Nick stood in his way.

Somewhere outside the altar room Nick could hear footsteps, drawing ever closer to the gateway. Hurrying across the stone floor Nick moved around the plinth. Ducking under the huge stone wing of the phoenix statue he slipped into the small gap behind it. Closing his eyes Nick held his breath, counting the number of steps until he would be found.

Then, suddenly, they stopped. Opening his eyes he found the grey stone of the statue staring back at him. Several more footsteps echoed around the room and then the creak of old hinges. The gate. In his haste to take the stone and get out of the cave he had left it open.

"Who do we have hiding in here then," rasped a cold voice as the gate clinked shut. "Could it be William? My old friend, why not come and show yourself? No? Perhaps someone else then. No matter, I will find you, sooner or later."

For several painstaking minutes that felt like hours Nick listened to the footsteps moving around the room, growing slowly closer to his hiding place.

This was the end, Nick thought, the least he could do now was try to distract him long enough until William could get to him.

"Come now, I have very little time for your foolish games," whispered the voice as a flickering shadow fell across the small gap between the statue and the wall.

CHAPTER FOURTEEN
RETURNING FROM THE SHADOWS

"Well, what do we have here?" rasped the man, his cold breath falling across Nick's face as he grabbed hold of his robe. With surprising strength he pulled Nick out from behind the statue, almost throwing him across the floor and into another statue. With a crash Nick hit the stone, wincing slightly.

"You're him aren't you," Nick said. It wasn't a question he posed to the cloaked man but a statement. With his hood drawn over his head, Nick couldn't gauge a reaction on the face that was hidden in the shadows.

"It would seem that my reputation has preceded me," Numquam whispered as he moved towards Nick once more. "But who are you? Has that foolish old man sent you in search of his long lost dreams?"

"Reputation?" spat Nick. "Of what a murderer? A coward, hiding behind your little friends?"

With a scream of rage and a flash a sword appeared in Numquam's hidden hand, slashing across the chest of Nick's robe faster than he thought was humanly possible.

"How dare you," snarled Numquam as he took hold of Nick again, throwing him to the floor. "I am the most powerful man to ever walk the earth, and you call me a coward? My friends, my followers, they stand beside me because they want to be on the winning side. To join me in the new world we will create. Tell me, where is your grandfather?"

"You already know that," Nick said, his voice low as he stared up at the man that towered over him.

"Dead," Numquam laughed. "Like all of those who have stood against me and now William sends you, a child to face me. Tell me Nick Harrison, who is the coward?"

"He'll be here soon. Then we will see if you really are the most powerful man on the earth," Nick said defiantly as he got to his feet again, taking a step towards Numquam.

"By which time I will have the stone in my possession and be long gone," Numquam whispered. With a swish of his cloak he headed towards the plinth where the fake stone sat.

Now was his chance, Nick thought as he slid the sword from its sheath. Turning, he strode forward, almost making it to a run before an invisible force hit him, knocking him off balance. With a clang his sword fell to the floor beside him, inches from his finger tips.

"You dare attack me while my back is turned," Numquam roared as he turned on Nick. "All this talk of cowardice, I thought you at least, would be brave enough to confront me face to face. It seems I was wrong."

Keeping his attention focused on Numquam, Nick tried to stretch his fingertips towards the hilt of the sword.

Just as he felt the cold of the metal it was blasted away by Numquam with a laugh.

"How can I take you on face to face when you have done nothing but hide behind that hood?" Nick asked as he glanced after his sword. After Numquam's last spell it lay in the shadows behind one of the towering stone phoenixes.

"In the world we live in we are all granted one last request before death," Numquam said, the sword appearing in his hand again. "Is this to be yours Nick?"

When Nick didn't respond Numquam raised his hands slowly towards the hood. With the sword still in his hand, Numquam lifted the black material, pushing it backwards. At first Nick thought it was a trick of the light but, as Numquam moved towards him, he wasn't so sure.

On the right side of Numquam's face the flesh had been ripped away, leaving behind pearly white bone. In its socket the white of his eye had almost disappeared behind bloodshot veins.

"Sometimes it pays to be certain what you are messing with, does it not?" Numquam asked quietly. "But it does not matter, I am immortal."

Standing over Nick now, Numquam raised the sword above his head, the blade sparkling in the firelight but that was not what drew Nick's attention. Set in the hilt of the sword was a black stone. Beneath him on the floor Nick's breath hitched, the muscles in his legs tensing as he prepared to launch himself towards his sword.

With a twitch in what was left of the skin on Numquam's face, the sword began to fall. Pushing against the ground Nick rolled aside, sliding across the smooth rock until he was behind the statue. As he moved he heard the crash as Numquam's sword struck the floor where Nick had been, sparks flying into the air.

The cold handle of the sword, Nick thought, would offer him some comfort and yet it didn't. He was sure that he didn't stand a chance against Numquam from what he had seen. Turning just in time he saw Numquam lunging at him and with some luck and a quick reaction he managed to deflect Numquam's blade away from him. However, the very tip of the blade caught the top of his arm on its way towards the statue. Nick felt the sting as it broke through his skin. Numquam had drawn the first blood.

Nick's head was spinning as he dodged a second lunge, ducking so that he now had Numquam pinned into the corner between the two statues. Half a smile appeared on Numquam's face as he watched Nick sidestep the blade as it slashed downwards.

Hours and hours of practice in the tunnels beneath Gladstow could never have prepared him for this. With the adrenaline running through his veins Nick tried to level the fight, mixing in several quick slashes to break up what had all been defensive so far.

On Numquam's lips the smile faltered slightly as the blade of Nick's sword came painfully close to drawing blood from his throat. The near miss did nothing but anger Numquam. His attacks began to come quicker and closer to the dark red robe that had already been slashed open twice. Backing away on the defensive, Nick glanced around for help.

As he took in the surroundings, Nick noticed that they had somehow worked their way into the centre of the altar room. The stone statues of the phoenixes towered over them. If he could just work his way back towards the stone, Nick thought as he dodged another attack, he could put it between them. If anything it would give him a moment of rest from the fight.

For several minutes Nick worked his way backwards, ducking and dodging Numquam's attacks. In the half of his face which showed any signs of emotion he could see the frustration building. His attacks were becoming more powerful and rash.

Seeing Numquam's sword swinging in his direction again he tried to step back but something stopped him. With a combination of the object behind his knees and his lean backwards to dodge the sword, Nick fell backwards on to the floor. The thing he had fallen over was the stone plinth. Nick watched as the Lava stone fell from the plinth, bouncing several feet to his left, his sword slipping from his sweaty fingers as he fell. Finally sensing his victory, Numquam stood before the plinth, the tip of the sword angled directly at Nick's heart.

"Move and I destroy it!" Nick shouted as he grabbed the sword, holding it aloft above the stone. Numquam froze, the sword still dangling above Nick. Breathing a sigh of relief Nick stared up at Numquam.

"You have fought well Nick," Numquam said quietly. "Michael would have been proud of his grandson."

"Don't tell me what he would have thought," Nick shouted. "You killed him!"

"These stones, have you ever seen the power that they are capable of?" asked Numquam quietly. "They have the power to heal cuts, burns, diseases. Hand over the stone Nick and I can heal him, save him. Then he can tell you how proud he would have been himself."

"You're lying! Why would you bring someone back who hated you even if you have a way?" Nick countered fiercely.

"I am giving you an offer that so many other people would jump at. A stone for the life of a loved one, it seems more than fair to me."

Slowly Nick reached out, grasping the fake stone in his hand, looking at it intently. He could give Numquam the fake stone to prove that he could not save his grandfather. Numquam would get what he wanted, or what he thought was what he wanted and Nick would get his proof. But if Numquam found out it was a fake his life would definitely be forfeit. It was such a perfect copy, he had compared them himself when he had arrived.

"You will bring him back if I give you the stone?" Nick confirmed.

"There is no fairer deal," Numquam replied calmly as he withdrew the sword that hung over Nick.

"Right here, right now, before my eyes?" Nick said, carefully laying out the terms of the deal.

"You have my word. The real stone for your grandfather's life," Numquam said.

"The real stone?" Nick questioned. Did he already know? How could he? All the time Numquam had been here the stone had been on the plinth. Maybe he saw Nick replace it, hiding in the shadows.

"Yes, the real stone," Numquam whispered. "The one you hold in your hand is a fake, a very convincing fake to someone who has never seen the stone."

"How do you know it's a fake?" Nick questioned curiously. If he managed to escape from here he would be able to pass the information on to William.

"Here," Numquam said, stretching out a hand to take the stone. "If this was the real stone it would not be chipped here, the result of it falling to the floor. The real stone would not be damaged by a fall, whether one foot or one thousand," explained Numquam, throwing the fake stone back to Nick who caught it.

"The real stone then . . ." Nick said, trailing off as he withdrew it from inside his robe. "I place the stone on the plinth, you perform whatever magic you need to do to heal my grandfather, then I let you leave with the stone."

"Very well," Numquam said, eyeing the stone as Nick withdrew his sword again. He didn't trust Numquam to keep his end of the deal to any extent.

As soon as Nick's hand was well away from the stone on the plinth Numquam lunged for it. With a crack Nick brought his sword down on Numquam's wrist.

"That wasn't the deal," Nick whispered as he leant forward to take the stone from Numquam's clutches.

All the time he had held the sword there he had not seen Numquam flinch in pain once and as he looked past the stone he saw why. Beneath the rip in the black material there was no flesh, just bone. The same pearly white to that on one half of his face.

Taking the two stones in one hand, Nick removed the sword from Numquam's wrist, his eyes locked with Numquam's blue ones the entire time. In a split second Numquam's sword was drawn again, the black stone in the hilt sparkling in the firelight, his attack coming moments later.

Throwing himself back against the statue Nick dodged the blade. Sword in one hand, stones in the other he watched as Numquam stepped up on to the plinth and down the other side. Slowly he stepped forwards, closing the space between himself and Nick. Praying that his last hope would work, Nick closed his eyes, lifting his arm and throwing both of the stones with all of the force he could muster.

The echoing clink of the stones across the stone floor told Nick that they were both bouncing away from them. Opening his eyes he saw Numquam lifting his sword, anger flowing through his eyes. Ducking under the sword Nick ran after the stones as they skidded towards the gateway. It felt as if he was getting away too easily and then the world flew out of focus as he was thrown off his feet.

Pain shot through Nick's body as he crashed to the floor, sliding to a stop at the base of one of the statues. Looking back towards the plinth Nick saw Numquam striding towards him. Between them lay rubble from one of the phoenixes that had been blasted apart by Numquam.

Using magic to carve a pathway towards Nick, Numquam ruthlessly launched pieces of stone to the sides of the room. Grabbing his sword from the floor Nick stood up, turning to face Numquam. Before he could take a step towards him he was thrown backwards on to the floor again.

Frantically scrambling to his feet again, Nick dived for cover behind another statue as a killing spell just missed him. Glancing back he saw it strike the gate. For a moment the altar room was silent, the gate glowing a golden colour and then, without warning the killing spell bounced from it, ricocheting around the room, destroying everything it hit. That was until it reached the phoenix that stood over the plinth where the stone had sat.

Taking cover from the falling rock, Nick coughed as dust filled his lungs. When the room fell quiet once more he glanced around the corner of the statue. Through the dust and debris Nick could see Numquam clambering to his feet again. Between them stood piles of rubble, three of the phoenixes almost completely destroyed, a wing missing from the one that stood at the back of the room.

Seeing his chance, Nick ran out from behind the statue, scrambling across the rubble with his sword in one hand, the other covering his head as a rainbow of coloured spells soared past him.

Throwing himself at Numquam, Nick knocked him off balance, his last spell, a killing spell, deflecting out over the water and into the darkness that surrounded them.

For several minutes they struggled, each trying to gain control over the other, their swords now lay forgotten amongst the rubble.

Finally Numquam took control and grabbed the first sword he saw by the hilt and swung it in Nick's direction. In an instant when he was sure he could see death there was an explosion of blue light above him. The blade of the sword, which Nick now saw was his own, split into two pieces. The hilt and a small part of the blade, that now resembled a dagger, remained in Numquam's hand. Bouncing away through the rubble was the second part of the blade.

Stretching, Nick's fingers closed around the hilt of Numquam's sword and with all his effort he pushed the man off of him. Getting to his feet he turned to face Numquam who stood before him holding what was left of Nick's sword.

The clang of metal on metal broke the silence in the cave. Using the distance to his advantage Nick began to attack, driving Numquam back across the rubble towards the edge of the stone floor.

For fifteen minutes they fought, neither able to take advantage of the others mistakes. Several times the tip of one of the blades would skim the flesh of the opponent and draw a little blood. Nick's plan to force Numquam to the edge of the water had worked and as he took his last step forward he kicked out at Numquam.

As his foot collided with Numquam's stomach the dagger like blade sliced across his thigh. Watching, Numquam fell backwards. Unable to keep his balance he tumbled into the water with a splash.

Slowly the water began to settle back into place as Nick examined the cut on his leg. It was far deeper than any of the others that either of them had dealt.

Looking around the partially destroyed room, Nick saw the ghost of the phoenix sitting on the plinth watching him. For a moment it remained quite still until the echoing voice filled the room. This time it had no prophecy for him. Just a single word: flee.

With a deafening crack it disappeared and Nick turned to the gate. To the side lay the two stones, indistinguishable from the distance he stood at. Taking in the advice the phoenix had given him, he scrambled forwards, hurrying over the rubble as fast as his injured leg would allow him.

Behind him Nick heard the splash of water but this time he didn't look back. His only thought now was to pick up the stones and get out of the altar room as fast as he could before Numquam resurfaced. As he moved he noticed that the room was slowly growing darker, the sound of the water louder now as if it was right behind him.

Spinning round, Nick found himself face to face with a wall of water that reached up as far as he could see. For a heartbeat it stayed exactly where it was. Then it broke. With the force of a small waterfall it crashed down on him, washing Nick aside along with rubble of all shapes and sizes.

For seconds that felt like minutes he couldn't breathe. The water was in control, and behind that Nick knew was Numquam.

Spluttering, Nick found himself lying on his side, the gate to the cavern just a few feet away. Beside it lay the two stones, resting where they had been left by the water as it began to retreat from the path. For the second time that day Nick found himself soaked to the bone.

"You fool!" Numquam shouted, his voice echoing. "You will end the same way as your grandfather. Rotting in a cave, forgotten by everyone you ever thought cared for you."

As he strode out of the darkness he bent down and took hold of the remains of Nick's sword. With the path now clear he could count the steps until Numquam reached him. Running a single, slender finger along the blade he considered Nick for a minute.

"Such a waste of a good fighter, you could have been so powerful," Numquam said. "Think of the power you could have had. With the stones no one would be a match for you. You could rule the world. All would cower before you, at your mercy."

"How do you know that I still can't be powerful?" Nick asked as he thought on Numquam's words. They were almost identical to those of the stone when he had first seen it. Could it be true? Could he really be that powerful? If he was supposed to be The Saviour he had come up short.

"You should have joined me when you had the chance, Nick," Numquam whispered as he closed the gap between them. Ten feet, nine, eight. "How can you be powerful when you are dead? You can't." Seven feet, six, five, four.

"Then finish it. Right here. Now!" Nick demanded as he rolled on to his back, making one last effort to get up. Three feet, two, one.

Above him, Numquam stood, turning the blade slowly between his fingers. Slowly he crouched down, placing a hand on Nick's shoulder, pushing him back to the ground. Nick locked eyes with Numquam as the remains of his sword hung above him, angled directly at his heart. Closing his eyes he waited for the pain, the unknowable amount of pain and then, nothing.

"You have fought valiantly," Numquam whispered. "When I say it I mean it, Michael would have been proud of you. What a shame you didn't live up to the expectations of the phoenixes.

"Get away from him!" With a deafening crash Nick heard metal breaking as it crashed to the stone floor. Eyes flying open he saw a glint of metal as Numquam's weapon flew from his hand, disappearing into the water with a splash.

Then Numquam, who had been so close by, had retreated as a jet of red light shot over Nick's head. Turning to the gateway, Nick looked for his saviour. Standing there, wireframe glasses slightly askew was William. In his hands, what Nick assumed, was his own staff.

"Sorry I'm late Nick," William said as he stepped past him to face Numquam. "That mist on the staircase got in the way. However, it looks like you managed to hold your own." With a crash William and Numquam began to fight, spells of all colours flying in every direction.

Chapter Fifteen
THE ESCAPE

"William, my old friend," Numquam said. "Finally you have decided to come out of hiding and face me."

"At no point was I hiding from you," William replied, twirling his staff in a complex movement that produced a deep purple spell. Following it with his eyes, Nick saw it strike Numquam in the chest, knocking him back several paces. "You merely lacked the ability to find me."

"But I did find you," Numquam shouted, drawing his own staff to block William's next spell.

"After forty years," William laughed, his smile faltering as a killing spell soared past his ear. On the floor beside him Nick felt the coldness of the killing spell. "Find some cover Nick!"

Not hesitating to take William's advice as another spell closed in, Nick ducked aside behind a pile of rubble, the stray spell streaking over his head with a crackle.

From his hiding place behind the rubble, Nick watched as William and Numquam's fight grew more and more ferocious with each passing minute. Spells were flying in each and every direction, a large number of those produced by Numquam were black. In his desperation to defeat William his spells were becoming less accurate. But still William matched him, ducking and dodging spells that would have been fatal as he tried to unbalance his opponent.

Around them, rock began to shatter and fall from the walls as the stray spells collided with the hard surfaces. Sneezing in the falling dust Nick caught sight of something, or two things, shimmering at the base of one of the remaining statues. Sitting on the cold floor, forgotten by everyone in the cave was the Lava stone and its replica.

Ducking low to avoid any of the stray spells Nick hurried towards the stones as fast as his injured leg would let him. Overhead, Nick heard the crackle of another killing spell. Numquam must have seen him making a move for the stones.

Dust and debris falling from the statue, Nick scooped up the stones and ducked into cover again.

Leaning against the cool stone Nick winced, the cut on his leg was becoming more painful. Pinpricks of blackness began to find their way into Nick's vision. He could feel himself slowly beginning to lose consciousness. Before him the world seemed to spin as he slid down the side of the statue to the floor.

"Nick!" William shouted. To Nick it seemed like he was miles away and if he hadn't been able to see a shaky outline of the old man standing close by, he would have believed it. "Are you alright?"

"I'm fine," Nick lied as he pushed himself slowly back to his feet.

"Go, get out of here," William said as he deflected another of Numquam's spells towards the ceiling.

With a bang that echoed around the cavern, rock began to fall from above them. The altar room was caving in on them. Another shout from William to leave drew Nick's attention back to the fight that was taking place. Numquam was beginning to take advantage of William's momentary distraction, forcing him backwards with a barrage of spells.

Deflecting another spell upwards, William drew the water from the pool behind Numquam once more, bringing it crashing down over him.

"Run, Nick!"

"What about you?" Nick called back as he watched Numquam slash his way through the water, banishing it towards William.

"I'll be right behind you," William promised as he blocked the advancing water to form a dark wall between them and Numquam.

Turning, Nick ran for the gate, only looking back when he heard a crash of water. The shield that William had placed between himself and Numquam must have broken. That proved to be true moments later when a wave of water rushed past Nick before cascading over the edge and into the chasm.

Behind him, Nick heard a hollow scream of anguish as Numquam saw that Nick had disappeared with the stone. A blaze of multicoloured spells added to the green torch light in the cavern as they soared past Nick, disappearing into the distance.

With a tremendous crash that resonated around the cave, the stairs beneath Nick's feet shook as another spell shot past him. Looking over his shoulder he saw Numquam standing by the gateway to the altar room, taking aim once more. Around him the ceiling was caving in but it seemed to go unnoticed by Numquam.

Pieces the size of boulders could be heard falling all around the cavern. Ahead of Nick, one piece struck the staircase breaking away part of several steps.

Suddenly Numquam's spells that continued to flash past him seemed hardly a threat at all. Surely it was only a matter of time before something fell from far above and broke away a piece of the staircase ahead of him. That or something would knock him from the stairs and into the darkness below.

With a crash that sent Nick tumbling down the last few steps and on to the platform, a boulder struck the stairs ahead of him. Looking up, a shaft of daylight had appeared high above in the ceiling. As light flooded into the cavern Nick saw rock falling on every side.

Around him the blue mist began to rise again, blocking out everything, including the sound of falling rock. Before Nick could get to his feet again something collided with the edge of the platform behind the mist, knocking it so that it became slightly slanted. When the cut on his thigh brushed against the stone his blood banished the mist. For a moment the platform grew lighter as the daylight filtered down once more. It only lasted a matter of seconds before a shadow fell over him.

Standing over him was Numquam; behind him a fiery portal burnt away the darkness. With a wave of a hand, it disappeared with a crack. Looking to the downward staircase Nick saw a large section missing where the falling boulder had hit it.

Numquam's arrival on the platform brought the mist from beneath the platform again, rising up to block out the surroundings once more. As it disappeared from view, Nick saw the other staircase crumbling, falling piece by piece into the darkness below.

"You see now Nick, it would have been far easier to hand over the stone and walk away," Numquam whispered as the mist closed in. Its presence didn't seem to bother him. "Instead, you will fall a thousand feet to your death. But, never fear, the world will know your story. Of how you fled rather than see out our duel and how your attempt led to your . . . tragic . . . death."

"Then why not just kill me now?" Nick asked, climbing to his feet to face Numquam. "You have your chance. I have nothing left to fight you with."

Before Numquam could reply a crash sent them both staggering as something out of sight struck the platform. Just about managing to keep his balance, Nick looked down at the platform. A jagged crack was slowly appearing in the rock, dividing it roughly in half, Nick standing one side of the crack, Numquam on the other.

Between them the two stones bounced, having slipped from Nick's hand when the platform had shook, coming to rest along the crack in the rock.

As the stone settled, Nick and Numquam locked eyes, Nick's soft brown ones finding something in Numquam's blue ones that stirred in the depths of his memories. When the cave around them fell silent for the first time Nick heard an echo, one that he now recognised to be his grandfather.

"For The Saviour to rise, he first must fall further than ever before."

With a bang the mist dispersed in an instant. Above them daylight was cascading down from where the high ceiling had caved in. For the first time in what felt like hours Nick could smell the fresh air that replaced the dank and dusty air that had filled the cave. Looking back at the stones the crack seemed to be widening, the platform crumbling beneath their feet.

Slowly the cracks spread outwards, crisscrossing until the platform looked as if it had been made of sand. In one moment it was there and then it wasn't, disintegrated into dust and they fell. Nick and Numquam along with the two stones, plunging into the darkness below.

Pain rushed through Nick's body as he turned his head to the side slightly. Yet he was still here, still alive. Somehow. Beneath him he could feel rock digging into his back.

On the insides of his eyelids he could see the last waking moment he had. The two stones hitting the floor, the real one bouncing away as the fake one exploded into a million pieces. Then there was nothing except darkness.

Opening his eyes slightly the light that fell from far above burned. Not far from where he lay he could see the Lava stone, sparkling in the light. Somewhere nearby he heard movement which pushed all thoughts of the stone from his mind. Unsure whether it was Numquam he lay perfectly still, watching the whole time through his eyelashes.

Unable to move without pain crippling his body, Nick could only watch as a cloaked figure took the stone from where it had come to rest. Examining it for several moments, Numquam pulled the hood over his head once more before turning to Nick. Slowly he walked over, a limp hampering one leg.

"Such a weak excuse for a challenge," Numquam spat. Staring down at Nick, he considered him for a moment. Then, with a wave of a hand a portal appeared and Numquam was gone, disappearing with a crack as the portal faded away.

For what felt like hours Nick stayed perfectly still, he could feel a thin line of blood trickling down the side of his face. Yet any attempt to wipe it away with a hand was met with pain that threatened to overtake him. The words that his grandfather had spoken suddenly echoed around his mind as they had echoed around the cavern earlier: For The Saviour to rise, he first must fall further than ever before.

As he thought on the words a light appeared in the distance, drawing closer to Nick. The light was far softer than the daylight that had forced Nick's eyes closed when he had seen it. Stopping some feet from Nick, he strained his eyes to see what it was. A man, but not just a man, he was far more than that. It was the ghostly imprint of his grandfather, come to find him as he lay amongst the rubble.

"The Saviour will rise from the rubble, just as a phoenix rises from the ashes," he spoke quietly, looking directly at Nick. Slowly he moved closer. "You have done well Nick."

"But he got away with the stone, it was all for nothing," Nick replied.

"I don't think it was all for nothing," Michael began. "At times I think he was more than lucky to get away how he did."

"How did I survive?" Nick asked. "It must have been a thousand feet we fell yet he got up and walked away."

"What really happened when the ritual went wrong for him no one knows," Michael said as he leaned in to examine the cut on the side of Nick's head. "All I know is that you should be proud of yourself. I know I am. So much was asked of you today, I just wish that I didn't have to ask any more of you, especially today."

"There's more?" Nick sighed, fighting the pain as he lifted an arm to wipe the blood that was running across the skin close to his eye.

"I'm afraid so," Michael nodded. "Although it can wait for a day when you have healed I must tell you now. I must ask you to find my remains. Your father does not speak of it but I know that it plagues him terribly. Find them and take them back to him. It will give him some peace of mind."

"Where are they?" Nick asked.

"He left them where I fell in The Temple of Immortality," Michael explained. "Although William knows what became of me he does not know where it was that I fell, see that he knows this."

"I will," Nick promised.

"One more thing before I go Nick," Michael added as he stood up once more. "Tell William that I am sorry, I almost stopped him but I was too late."

"He doesn't blame you," Nick called after the retreating ghostly figure.

"Goodbye Nick," Michael said, his voice fading away into the distance. "At least for now."

Silently Nick watched the ghostly glow disappear as exhaustion began to creep over him, his eyelids dropping, leading him back into darkness.

Chapter Sixteen

NICK'S CHOICE

Somewhere far away Nick heard a shout, a shout of a name. Then came the sound of footsteps, drawing closer. With a crash a door opened and within seconds Nick felt a weight on his chest, a warm breathing weight. The mass that still remained hidden behind Nick's eyelids began to sob gently. As tears fell on to the skin of his neck, Nick opened his eyes only to be met by darkness.

"Rose?" whispered Nick. His voice was croaky, due to all the dust in the cave, Nick was sure. At the sound of her name the darkness disappeared, replaced by Rose's face, her black hair hanging haphazardly around her shoulders.

"Nick," Rose exclaimed, throwing her arms around his neck and clinging on for dear life. "I thought you were dead."

"I will be in a minute if you don't let me breathe," Nick whispered. That was another thing Nick knew Rose for. Firstly her love of books and secondly her suffocating hugs.

"Sorry," Rose laughed as she withdrew her arms from around his neck and he couldn't help but join in. It was moments like this that he knew had kept him fighting in the cave, Nick thought as he looked around his room. It was exactly how he remembered it, except for one thing. On the small bedside table was a black, leather bound book.

Their uncontrollable laughter must have alerted someone in the next room to the change in Nick's condition. Behind Rose, who was now sat up on Nick's bed, the door creaked open.

"What happened?" Rose asked.

"I think that is a question we would all like to know the answer to," William said as he appeared in the doorway behind Nick's parents.

Slowly Nick began to recount his story, answering questions when they were asked, the majority by Rose. It quickly became obvious that William had not told her his part of the story. Carefully he worked around the details of his encounters with the ghostly imprint of his grandfather. Those, he had decided, were for William and his father alone.

"A thrilling story," William concluded when Nick fell silent, his voice hoarse from recounting the events in the cave. "But to live it, quite terrifying I am sure."

"William," Mrs Harrison addressed, turning to face the old man. "You said that you would like to speak with Nick."

"If I may," William replied. "That is if Nick is up to it," he added.

With a confirming nod from Nick, Rose reluctantly got to her feet, waving goodbye as she followed Mrs Harrison from the room. Nick was left alone now with William and his father.

"There's more," Nick said quietly before either of the other men could speak. "Something else happened in the cave that day."

"Would you like me to call your mother and Rose back?"

"No," Nick said, sounding slightly harsher than he had meant to. "They can't know."

"What happened Nick?" William asked, mirroring Nick's quiet tone.

"There was someone else there, in the cave," Nick said. "Well, there in a way."

"What do you mean?" Mr Harrison asked.

"There was someone else in the cave, an imprint of someone who was there a long time ago," Nick began. "Someone we all know to be dead."

"Nick?" William asked cautiously.

"He asked me to tell you that he was sorry," Nick said, turning to William. "By the time he got there Numquam had already performed the ritual."

"You spoke to him, you spoke to Michael?"

"Yes," Nick whispered.

"What happened to him?" Mr Harrison queried.

"Numquam murdered him after he completed the ritual," Nick explained.

"Do you know what happened to his body?" Mr Harrison asked.

"Numquam left him where he fell," Nick said. "I'm going to find him. I'll bring him back."

"In time Nick," William assured him. "For now you must rest. Your wounds need time to heal before you do anything like that."

"But-"

"Nick," Mr Harrison cut him off sharply. "It has been forty years, a little longer won't make any difference. When you have recovered, then by all means I will not stop you."

"You need to listen to your father, Nick," agreed William. With a sigh Nick conceded defeat, there was no way he was going to win this argument.

"What are we supposed to do now though? We can't just sit here," Nick sighed. Frustration was starting to get the better of him.

"There isn't anything we can do," William insisted. "This isn't something we can rush into, we need a plan."

"He has the stone though," Nick explained looking between William and his father as they exchanged a quick glance, William shuffling his feet uncomfortably. "What?"

"You remember when I showed you the somnium ostendo sum spell, the one that showed you the dream when Numquam broke into my house?" William asked.

Nick remained silent, acknowledging William with a nod that told him to continue.

"There was something else that happened that night," William said, hurrying to continue as Nick began to sit up angrily. "Something that I did not discover until we returned to Gladstow."

"What was it?" Nick demanded.

"Do you remember what the sword Numquam wielded against you in the altar room looked like?" William asked.

"Yes, it had a black stone in the hilt, just like the one in the room beneath . . ." Nick trailed off as he realised what William was implying. "It was the same sword?"

"It was. Do you know what happened to it?" there was a sense of desperation in William's pleading voice now.

"I think he took it with him," Nick recollected. "I don't really remember. Was it important?" somehow Nick already thought he knew the answer to his question.

"The stone embedded in the hilt of the sword was the Death stone," William explained. "When the three of us were searching for the stones we fashioned a weapon. In the hilt we placed the first stone we found, the most powerful of the seven as we had concluded from our translations of ancient texts relating to the legend."

"When we returned to Gladstow I couldn't find the sword. If what you say is true then he now possesses two of the stones, including the most powerful one."

"Then surely we need a plan," Nick said. "Maybe we can get to him before he gets too strong."

"To go after him on your own would be suicide!" Mr Harrison exclaimed.

"But I already fought him, I know what I'm up against," Nick said, trying desperately to justify his point.

"Nick, you need to understand, this is far bigger than you can comprehend," William insisted. "Far bigger than any of us can comprehend. We have to have a plan or we don't stand a chance."

"What is the plan then?" Nick asked harshly. Their conversation seemed to have only been going round in circles.

"When he realises that the other stones are here in Gladstow, he will come for them with nothing short of an army. He will want to make sure that no one can stand in his way," William said. "Now that he knows about you he will assume that you will be close to me. You will be in a greater danger than anyone can know."

"So w-" Nick began, pausing as William raised a hand to silence him.

"That Nick is why you will not be here when he comes," William whispered.

"But-"

"Nick, please listen to me," William begged. "Originally this was all about protecting the stones, and in some way it still is, but we have other priorities now. You are our best chance to end this once and for all."

"There will come a time for you to fight; we need to make sure that you are ready for that day when it comes. I know that you would rather deal with this now. Believe me, if I thought we could beat him now and save all the innocent lives that will be lost then we would leave now. Sometimes sacrifices need to be made, as much as we regret them."

"Where do you want me to go if I can't stay here?" Nick sighed. Something about William's speech told Nick that there would be no other way.

"I have already made arrangements for that," William revealed. "I have a contact living in the city that I could trust with my life. He has agreed to take you into his household and look after you for the foreseeable future. He lives not too far from the library that you like to spend time in. I also believe he has a daughter around your age, perhaps she can help you with your training."

"I thought we had finished with the sword training though?" Nick asked recalling the conversation they had had at William's house before heading to Akraneimacy.

"That brings me to another thing," William said. "Could you pass Nick the book please Mr Harrison."

Moving around to the side of Nick's bed, Mr Harrison picked up the small, black, leather bound book that sat on the bedside table. Passing it to Nick he returned to his place by the door.

"I know that I said I was going to teach you everything that you would need to know. Well, with the change in the situation it will not be as easy as we hoped," William said. "Your grandfather left this book in my possession the night he left to find Numquam, perhaps if I had known where he was going I would have gone with him."

"What is it?" Nick asked as he opened the book to the first page which was blank.

"Throughout the years we spent searching for the stones you grandfather recorded everything, from translations and locations to spells and theories," William explained. When Nick turned to the next page he saw what William had been talking about. Page after page had been filled with scribbled writing and rough diagrams.

"Why is the first page blank though?" Nick asked curiously as he finished flicking through the pages. As he turned back to the beginning the edge of one of the pages sliced across his thumb, a single drop of blood falling from the paper cut on to the first page.

"A question I asked your grandfather myself," William replied. "He never told me, he just said there was a reason." As William finished speaking the drop of blood faded from the page, replaced by the familiar untidy scrawl that Nick recognised as his grandfathers. Slowly letters began to materialise, letters became words, words became sentences and then, as suddenly as it had begun it stopped.

"William," Nick said quietly as he held up the book on the page that had been blank. "It isn't blank anymore, look."

"Nick, what do you mean, the page is blank," Mr Harrison asked wearily with a glance at William.

"Are you sure Nick? I don't see anything either."

"Yes," Nick replied turning the book round again. "It's here, right at the top of the page.

"Whatever it is Nick, neither of us can see it," William said gesturing to himself and Mr Harrison.

"But surely you can see it, it's written right here in ink," Nick said pointing to the words on the page as he showed the book to William and his father again.

"I wonder . . ." William muttered to himself as he ran a hand through his grey hair. "There is one possible explanation but it would be a long shot, not to mention very difficult to achieve. There is one enchantment that I know of that could create a phenomenon similar to this. What do the words say Nick?"

Looking down at the page Nick began to read; "Heed my words Saviour. Through everything there is a balance of good and evil. One must not exceed the other for them to exist together. In a time far from now the balance will be unsettled. The evil that had lain dormant in the shadows will make its way to the forefront after the side of good has taken its fall. It rests with you, Saviour to restore the balance. If the Saviour should fall only an act of unspeakable evil will resolve the balance between good and evil, the cost of this is a soul, tainted forever. Then it's signed by 'The Adventurer'," Nick finished, as a stunned silence fell around the room, all of them lost in their own thoughts.

"Your grandfather . . ." William whispered. "He knew all along." William's face seemed to fall with disappointment as he realised the secret that had been kept from him. "He knew! I could have stopped this if he had told me the truth!"

"William," Nick said quietly as the old man fell quiet after his outburst. "Maybe there was a reason he didn't tell you. What would have happened if you had both gone after him and neither of you had come back. We would be even worse off than we are now. You said it yourself; sometimes we have to make sacrifices we regret."

"You are right Nick, of course. I am sorry for my outburst," William apologised.

"Where do we go from here?" Nick asked, waving away William's apology.

"We will prepare over the next few days. I think it would be safe for you to remain here and spend Christmas with your family. Besides, I believe there is one tradition you would not want to miss," William said.

"The decorating of the church for the Christmas service? I haven't missed it?" Nick asked hurriedly. For as many years as anyone in Gladstow could remember it had been tradition that the children of the village would decorate the church with flowers for the midnight mass service. No one was sure how or when it had started but it was something that had always continued, ending for each child in the year of their eighteenth birthday. Although he had never really thought about it, Nick would have been disappointed if he had missed his last chance to decorate the church.

"You woke at just the right time," Mr Harrison said with a smile. "I think, if you hurry, you might make it just in time to help the other children."

"I will let you get ready Nick, I'm sure you don't want to be late," William explained as he moved towards the door.

"We will speak later to discuss things to make sure you are ready to head to the city in the New Year.

"Will I be alright to go?" Nick asked his father as the door swung shut behind William.

"I think you can manage it," Mr Harrison said with a laugh. "I don't think I could deny you your last chance to decorate the church, or Rose a chance see you," he added as an afterthought.

After Mr Harrison had left the room Nick fought off the pains of his aching body to get dressed. Pulling on the thick robe that he had been presented with on Akraneimacy he slipped the black book into one of the pockets. He planned to show it to Rose later and see what she could make of it.

With the torn robe wrapped around him, Nick hurried through the house and out into the snow covered street, heading for the church in the distance.

CHAPTER SEVENTEEN

MISTLETOE AND ROSES

It wasn't long after Nick had left the warmth of the house that he heard the sound of children talking and laughing. While walking through the village he had not heard or seen anyone. He couldn't blame them really; they were all staying inside to get away from the freezing temperatures that had settled on Gladstow.

Arriving at the church, Nick pushed the heavy oak door open, welcomed by the sound of murmured voices and warmth from the small fireplace. Inside the church some thirty children had gathered, their ages ranging across ten years or so.

With a creak the church door swung shut behind Nick. Those who had been closest to the door, decorating with the stacks of red and white roses that had been magically enchanted to survive the cold winter and remain in flower, looked round to see who had joined them.

In seconds the chatter that had filled the church died away as if it had been sucked from the room, leaving behind an empty coldness. From the middle of the crowd a boy with short, curly blonde hair who must have been fourteen or fifteen spoke up.

"Welcome back Nick."

"It's good to be back," Nick replied. He could sense that there was a question the blonde boy was burning to ask along with many others.

"Are the stories true?" asked a younger girl who, going by her curly blonde hair, Nick guessed to be the boy's younger sister. "You fought him?"

"Yes, the stories are true," Nick confirmed with a nod. With a cheer the children in the church surrounded him, congratulations flying in from every side. Though they were only children they all knew the stories of the raids on towns and villages. From the crowd though, Nick could see that someone was missing. Rose.

Looking over the heads of the younger children Nick saw her sitting on a rickety, flower laden table. In front of Rose stood her younger sister Katie. She was Rose in miniature, her long black hair hanging in a loose ponytail unlike Rose's.

As the excitement died down, Nick eased his way through the crowd towards Rose and her sister, catching snatches of their conversation.

"I'm sure he'll make it to the service later," Katie said quietly. It seemed they had both been oblivious to what had been going on in the rest of the church.

"What and miss this? Not a chance," said Nick. Jumping back in surprise, Katie revealed Rose who lifted her head slowly at the sound of his voice.

"You made it!" Rose said excitedly as she leapt off the table, scattering bundles of flowers across the floor, throwing her arms around him.

"Of course I made it," Nick whispered into her ear as he returned her hug. "You know I hate being stuck in bed with nothing to do."

"I don't want to think about what would have happened if you hadn't turned up Nick," Katie piped up. "She's been sitting here pulling her hair out since we got here. We haven't done any decorating at all."

"Well I think we should clear up this mess before we start," laughed Nick as he gestured to the flowers that littered the floor around them.

"I'm sorry," apologised Rose.

"For what?" Nick and Katie asked together.

"Ruining the day for you, Katie."

"Nonsense Rose. You're my sister. It's my job to make you feel better. So I think you should drop it now or you will be ruining the day," Katie said angrily before turning and with a bunch of flowers in hand, headed to the far side of the church. As she left Nick could have sworn he saw a satisfied smile cross her lips.

"She has a point," said Nick. His comment was met with raised eyebrows by Rose.

"Be quiet and help me pick these up," Rose muttered warningly.

"Sorry," Nick replied. As he bent down to help he felt the weight of the black leather book in his pocket. It could wait, he thought, at least until later.

In the early hours of Christmas morning the congregation of Gladstow spilled from the small church into the snowy graveyard. Nick had decided to wait until after the service to tell Rose about the book and William's plan. That was where he found himself now, leaning on the snow covered picket fence beside Rose, the dull murmur of conversation carrying on the cold night air across the dark graveyard.

"The flowers looked amazing this year," Nick said. "I can't remember a year that they have been better."

"I'm glad you liked them," Rose said absently as she pulled the white rose, that had been entwined in her hair, loose. Since the decorating of the church she had returned home to get ready for the service. When she had re-emerged she was wearing a long blue dress that perfectly matched the colour of her eyes, the single white rose entwined in her hair. "I remember picking them for William to enchant while you were in the city."

"William wants me to return to the city in the New Year," Nick said slowly, trying to gauge Rose's reaction.

"Again?" Rose asked.

"He thinks it would be best," Nick explained. "William is convinced that he will come here for the stones. Numquam already believes that I am dead, if I'm not here I can prepare without worrying about him looking for me."

"Maybe I'll get a chance to visit," said Rose thoughtfully as she stared out across the lake, the dark water forming a mirror that reflected the broken cloud.

"William also gave me this," said Nick, withdrawing the leather bound book from his pocket and handing it to Rose. "He said it belonged to my grandfather"

"It looks interesting," said Rose slowly as she flicked through the pages.

"When I first looked at it I got a paper cut off one of the pages, my blood dropped on the first page," explained Nick. "When it did it revealed words that neither William nor my father could see."

"I don't know how they can't see it, its right here," said Rose. Looking over her shoulder he read the passage again with her.

Heed my words Saviour. Through everything there is a balance of good and evil. One must not exceed the other for them to exist together. In a time far from now the balance will be unsettled. The evil that had lain dormant in the shadows will make its way to the forefront after the side of good has taken its fall. It rests with you, Saviour to restore the balance. If the Saviour should fall only an act of unspeakable evil will resolve the balance between good and evil, the cost of this is a soul, tainted forever.

The Adventurer

"What do you think it all means?" asked Nick as she handed the book back to him.

"Maybe it is some kind of prophecy-" Rose began.

"Not another one," sighed Nick in exasperation.

"I could be wrong though," said Rose, trying her best to look upbeat. "Yes it does look like a prophecy but," Rose paused, raising a hand to silence Nick. "It looks like a prophecy but it's as if it isn't complete."

"What makes you think that it isn't complete?" asked Nick.

"Look at where it is signed," Rose pointed out.

"The bottom of the page?" asked Nick, unsure of the point she was trying to make.

"If you wrote something only a few lines long why would you sign it at the bottom of the page?" Rose asked. When Nick remained clueless she continued. "It's as if there is supposed to be more written here. Like it's only revealing what has already happened."

"Great, a prophecy that re-writes itself," Nick sighed. "Just what we needed with so many other prophecies around."

As they looked out over the lake the moon broke through the cloud, reflecting off the surface. On the page of the book that they had been reading more words began to appear, momentarily unnoticed by Nick and Rose.

"There's more, in the book," Rose pointed out after a minute of silence.

Looking down Nick saw the words that had appeared only moments ago. Together they began to read again.

The Saviour, the one who carries the weight of the future on his shoulders. He is strong and brave and will face trials that he must overcome if he is to stand a chance of coming face to face with evil.

The Sage, her knowledge is her power. Though her attention may wander her heart will beat and stay true to The Saviour until the end.

The Light, she will have an unbreakable spirit and in times of darkness her insight will light the path for The Saviour.

In the hands of these three lies the hope of the world. This book will reveal what is to come and what has transpired.

It can and will change. The future can be changed by sheer force of will, destiny cannot be denied.

"What is that all supposed to mean?" Nick asked as Rose took the book from his hands.

"I think it means that I'm involved in it whether you like it or not," said Rose with a satisfied smile.

"I've always included you in this," Nick said slowly.

"William hasn't though," she pointed out, handing the book back to him before she turned away. "Surely you noticed that when something happens he never tells me about it. What about the night he sent you looking for the lynx? What about the day when he took you to get your staff? What about when you went looking for that stone?"

"Rose, I'm sorry," Nick called after her as she began to walk away towards the archway that led out of the graveyard.

"Of course you are Nick," Rose shouted over her shoulder as she carried on walking. "You always say you're sorry but when something new happens you never tell me."

"I never get the chance," Nick said as he ran to catch up with her, stopping her under the archway. "Everything happens so quickly and I get whisked off to some other place."

"Strange how that seems to work out isn't it," Rose spat. "What a shame I'm involved in this now. I guess you have to tell me everything now."

"When have I not told you everything I know?" asked Nick taking her by the shoulders and forcing her to look at him. "I may not have a choice in this now but that doesn't mean that I like the idea of you being involved in this. I don't want you to get hurt . . . or worse. You're my best friend Rose."

"I always seem to be the best friend," Rose sighed as she looked up. "There's something that I don't understand though."

"What is it?"

"You always jump feet first into everything, always," Rose whispered. "Why not this?"

Looking up, Nick saw what she had been staring at. Attached to the arch above them was a small bunch of mistletoe. When he looked back Rose was removing the necklace, from which a phoenix shaped charm hung, which was hanging around her neck.

"I found this when I was looking through my father's things," she said quietly. "If you're going to the city I want you to take it with you."

"Rose-" Nick began as he looked back at her. Before he could finish she slipped her arms around his neck, pulling him closer.

For the briefest of moments his brown eyes met her blue ones and then her lips were against his. In those few seconds he was oblivious to the rest of the world around him as he kissed her back. And then it dawned on him. He froze, easing her away from him.

"Rose," Nick whispered. "We can't. He's going to come here looking for the stones. If he knew he would find you. Use you against me as long as I'm alive. I'm sorry."

Leaving his words to hang in the air he turned, walking away from her and back towards the village.

"Nick, I-" Rose called after him, breaking off into a whisper when he didn't look back. He didn't hear her whispered words or see the single tear slide down her cheek, slowly freezing in the cold night air.

Alone Nick walked through the dark deserted streets of Gladstow. He was just letting his feet choose the path he followed while he was lost in thought. Engrossed in his thoughts he didn't hear the door of one of the houses open, he didn't hear the footsteps on the cobbled street. Not until he stood at the edge of the lake looking out over the water did he realise there was someone with him.

"Nick, what are you doing out here?"

"Thinking," Nick replied without looking round. He recognised the voice but Katie was not the person he would have picked to talk about what had happened at the church.

"Where did you and Rose go?" Katie asked.

"We were in the graveyard talking," Nick explained. "William gave me a book that belonged to my grandfather earlier today. I was showing it to Rose."

"Then what happened?" she questioned, moving to stand next to Nick.

"She said I always jump into things," Nick explained. "Then she asked me why I didn't with this."

"Nick, I know my sister," Katie began. "Rose cares, more than you know, I think. Twice you disappeared without a trace and when you came back you ended up unconscious for days at a time. Do you know how many of those days she spent waiting for you to wake up, praying you would wake up?"

Silently Nick shook his head; he was still staring out over the water. It was all he could do not to look at Katie. She looked too much like Rose and right now Rose wasn't the person he wanted to see.

"All of them. Maybe you should think on that before the next time you see her," said Katie. "Goodnight, Nick."

Without another word to him she turned and left, leaving him alone. His thoughts were his only companions for now. Seizing on that thought he looked down on the book in his hand. If it was supposed to reveal the future to him then why did it not warn him of this, why was it not revealing what would happen next.

Opening the book to the first page he looked down at the words. Had his grandfather written this all those years ago? How had he known? Who was The Light?

Slowly his thoughts turned to his return to the city. Whatever William's plan was Nick needed to trust him now. Perhaps it would be a chance for him to get away from the prophecy, at least for a little while.

CHAPTER EIGHTEEN
A BIGGER BEGINNING

From an explosion of green sparks, Nick emerged, his sheepskin bag dangling from his shoulder. Standing before him was a small church, not all that different from the one in Gladstow, where he had revealed William's plan to Rose just a week ago, the roof covered in a thin layer of snow.

Reluctantly, Nick had said goodbye to Rose earlier that morning before meeting with William at the old man's house.

Once again Nick found himself in the city, in the spot he had departed from last September. That had been a better time by far, he reminisced as he turned to face the graveyard. That was when stories of Numquam Intereo had been just that, stories. And now, here he stood, on the first day of the New Year, as arranged by William, with one battle behind him and a collection of scars across his body.

Taking the weaving path between the graves and mausoleums, Nick headed for the cobbled street that sat on the other side of the high, iron railings. Shivering slightly, Nick pulled his robe tightly around him. It had been patched up as best as it could be. The street was silent and deserted. To Nick it seemed quite unusual. With the watery sun beating down as it neared midday he thought he would have at least seen someone walking around, going about their business of the day.

Withdrawing the directions that William had given him, from his pocket, Nick set off along the street. On one side the terraced houses curved with the street as the graveyard narrowed. Sighing, Nick walked on with a slight limp. Although the cut on his thigh was healing, it was still immensely painful.

Twenty minutes later Nick reached the end of William's instructions. In the distance he could just make out the outline of the building that he knew to be the library. Far behind him the church and the graveyard had disappeared. Turning to face the house at the end of the terrace, number eight, Nick approached the black door. Taking the brass knocker, which looked distinctly like a phoenix, he knocked three times.

For several moments there was nothing and then, following a rush of movement the door creaked open an inch or so, a soft brown eye appearing in the gap.

"Nick Harrison," Nick said quietly. "William Stokes sent me. I'm looking for George Williams."

"You found me then," a man's voice replied. Slowly the door swung open to reveal the owner of the eye. Standing there was a man in his early forties. "George Williams," he said, extending a hand to Nick. "When William spoke of his plan I was more than enthusiastic to get the opportunity to meet you."

"Well, here I am," said Nick as George stepped aside to allow him into the house.

"Come on through Nick," George said as he led the way into a large room. The walls were all plain, the furniture all made in the same style. One thing that stood out to Nick though was the fireplace. Sitting on the mantelpiece was a large figurehead of a dragon. As Nick examined it, it appeared to be made of glass. "Make yourself comfortable."

"Thank you," said Nick appreciatively as he sat down next to the roaring fire, lowering his bag to the floor.

"So, the way I heard it from William you beat Numquam Intereo in a fight recently," George said as he sat down opposite Nick.

"I wouldn't say I beat him," said Nick. "He got away with what he came looking for."

"You being alive is a victory," interrupted a voice from the doorway. "There are very few people who have managed to walk away from a fight with Numquam Intereo."

Looking towards the doorway Nick saw a girl standing there, leaning against the door-frame. She looked to be around the same age as Nick. This must have been the daughter William had told him about. As she pushed her long brown hair over one shoulder she stepped into the room with a smile. The first thing Nick noticed was her eyes, soft brown and yet they burned like there was a fire behind them.

"This is Lucy, my daughter," George said to Nick. "This is Nick, William asked us to give him a safe haven in the city while . . ."

Before George could continue there was the sound of a bell ringing close by. Looking round Nick saw the dragon on the mantelpiece glowing bright red. Rising from his seat George moved towards it. For a moment he stood in silence, staring at it.

"You will have to forgive me," said George hurriedly. "I have to go. Lucy can you stay here and help Nick get settled in. I'm sure you can explain."

"But-" Lucy began before she was cut off by her father.

"No buts Lucy," he called as he ran from the room. "I can fill you in when I get back." A few seconds later they heard the sound of the door slamming behind George.

"I'm sorry," said Nick quietly. "What just happened?"

"My father just left me here to deal with you while he gets to go investigate what just happened," Lucy said spitefully turning to face the fire.

"Sorry."

"It's not your fault Nick," sighed Lucy as she turned to look at him.

"What just happened that he needed to investigate?" asked Nick.

"We are part both part of an underground society that works to combat Numquam's forces," Lucy explained. "William is a part of it as well."

"Was this his plan all along then?" Nick asked. "To bring me here so I could join an underground society."

"Maybe, I didn't know anything about a plan if there was one," replied Lucy truthfully. "From what I've heard of the prophecies you are supposed to be 'The Saviour'. Welcome to the resistance, Nick."

"Can you tell me more about this society?" asked Nick, as Lucy took the seat opposite him that George had earlier vacated.

"I guess so, there isn't much else we can do until my father gets back," said Lucy. "The Heart of the Dragon was set up years ago after Numquam attacked the city on his search for immortality. Since then the society has been trying to counter Numquam and his followers, trying to predict his next move. He always seems to stay one step ahead of us though."

"I know that feeling," said Nick, thinking about how Numquam had appeared in the cavern just hours after he and William had arrived.

"William said I was supposed to help you with something," Lucy said. "Something to do with a book?"

"He must have meant this," Nick replied as he withdrew the black, leather bound book from his pocket. "It belonged to my grandfather apparently. William gave it to me just before Christmas."

"Can I look?" she asked. Not waiting for a reply she took the book from him, her hand brushing against his for a second.

For several minutes she sat in silence, flicking from one page to the next as she examined what Nick's grandfather had written. While her attention was focused on the book Nick looked around the room. The room was lit by the dull light of candles as well as the fire that was burning hungrily around the logs.

"I should be able to help with this," Lucy said, breaking the silence. "Although I have no idea what this part is about." Looking back at Lucy, Nick saw the page the book was open on as she held it out to him. Staring back at him were the words that had appeared when he had shown the book to Rose.

Rose, he thought, since they had gone their separate ways in the churchyard they had only spoken once. That had been earlier in the day. There had been no mention of what had happened that night since then and Nick was more than happy to keep it that way.

"You can see that as well?" Nick said thoughtfully. "That's strange; the only other person who could read it was Rose."

"Who's Rose?" Lucy asked curiously, her interest drawn from the book.

"A friend of mine in Gladstow," said Nick in an offhand tone.

"So I guess the whispers were true then," Lucy said quietly. "The Saviour has come."

"Whispers?"

"For some time now there have been rumours spreading amongst the members of The Heart of the Dragon," Lucy said. "They were only whispers though, no one knew for sure and they weren't going to announce anything without proof."

"What do you think about it all?" asked Nick.

"I don't know," Lucy replied. "Maybe we finally have someone on our side that stands a chance against him. Well, that's from what William has told everyone."

Falling into an uneasy silence, Nick and Lucy waited for George to return with news of what had happened.

It turned out that they didn't have to wait long for George to return. When he returned he moved swiftly towards the fireplace. For a moment he stood in front of the dragon on the mantelpiece. From where Nick was sitting he couldn't see what George was doing. When he turned to face them there was a grave look on his face.

"There was an attack," George said quietly.

"Where?" Lucy demanded, getting to her feet.

"On the far side of the city," he replied. "They say they were going from house to house looking for people working against them."

"Did they capture anyone?" asked Lucy.

"Capture? No, we only found out from someone who escaped," George explained. "They weren't killing them; they were destroying them, tearing them apart like a pack of wild animals. The message is that they are looking for anyone with an alliance to The Heart of the Dragon and they will kill them. It is rumoured that Numquam himself walks the streets of the city wielding a sword with a black stone in its hilt, cutting down anyone who even tries to oppose him."

"What do we do?" Nick said as he stood up with them.

"We stay here, there is nothing we can do for any of them," George said. "Especially with you here now Nick."

"Is it always like this?" asked Nick. "Not much news gets to Gladstow and what does is normally so distorted by the time it gets there that there is no truth left in it.

"It can be bad at times," said Lucy, running her hand through her hair. "I don't think it's ever been this bad before though."

"From time to time they attack a village or a town but they hardly ever come to the city," George said. "I've never heard of them going from house to house and killing anyone that gets in the way."

"William said this was bigger than we all knew," Nick said as he walked towards the small window that overlooked the street. "I guess I see what he meant now."

In the distance Nick could see plumes of black smoke billowing into the sky, an orange glow of fire reflecting back down off the grey clouds that stretched to the horizon. It was becoming too much for him to take and he turned away, looking to George and Lucy.

"I can't just sit here and let people die," Nick said. "I'm the one who is supposed to defeat him."

"Nick! You can't just go out there," Lucy said, frustrated. "You don't even have a weapon; he would blast you to pieces. It would be suicide."

"Blasted to pieces . . ." George said slowly. "That's it! Wait here, I know someone who might be able to help us."

Kissing his daughter on the forehead, George brushed past Nick as he ran from the room. From the hallway the sound of the door slamming shut for the second time broke the silence that had been left in the room. All Lucy and Nick could do was look at each other perplexed as to what George's idea was.

Chapter Nineteen
THE GHOST OF THE PHOENIX

The half an hour that Lucy and Nick sat in silence waiting for George to return seemed to last an eternity. Finally when they heard the front door creak open they both jumped to their feet, running into the hallway.

In the dim light Nick saw two men following George. Without a word he ushered them from the hallway until they stood grouped around the fire. As the firelight flickered across their faces Nick could see that the two men were brothers. At a distance they could have passed as identical twins. However, up close one had darker hair than the other.

Before any of them could speak there was a flash of lightning that illuminated the room. Moment's later rain began to thunder on the roof and bounce off the cobbled streets. In seconds the street looked more like a river, torrents of water rushing passed the window.

"Nick, I would like to introduce you to Peter and Andrew Carr," George said. "Andrew works for Ellison's Gas, Coal and Light Company. They are based in the area of the city that The Dark Movement is currently attacking."

"We believe we may have a plan," Andrew said stepping closer to the fire. The expression on his face was deadly serious, his brown eyes focused on Nick as he spoke. "I don't need to warn you of how dangerous this will be. If we can lure Numquam and his forces towards the gas plant all it would take was a stray spell to cause an explosion."

"Using my brother's knowledge of the plant we have identified a small concrete bunker which would be able to withstand the explosion," said Peter, stepping up to his brother's side.

"All we need is a way to lure him in our direction though," George said thoughtfully.

"Leave it to me," Nick replied. "I'll think of something."

"I think we are all set then," George said. "Andrew, if you would lead the way."

As they were about to leave the room Nick pulled Lucy back. Quickly he withdrew the book that William had given him before Christmas.

"Lucy, take this," he whispered. "If something happens to me I need you to take this to Gladstow, give it to William."

Nodding she took the book from him. Taking a blue robe from the hook beside the door she pushed the book into an inside pocket before putting the robe on.

Half an hour of winding back streets was what it had taken the five of them to reach Ellison's Gas, Coal and Light Company without getting caught up in any of the fighting. Bodies had littered the streets they had passed. Some belonged to men and women, others children who had been trying to escape. One that Nick knew would haunt him was a child who had attempted to escape on a bike. All that was left now were charred remains, still clinging to the bike that had been blasted several feet up into a tree.

While George and Peter watched for anyone coming up behind them, Andrew unlocked the heavy iron gates, ushering Nick and Lucy in ahead of him.

"Any thoughts on how we can draw his attention?" asked Lucy as she and Nick walked towards the large gas container.

"I don't know," Nick said, one hand twirling the phoenix charm, which Rose had given to him, between his fingers. "We need something like a flare, something that will go high enough in the sky to attract his attention."

"How are we doing with attracting his attention?" called George as he joined Nick and Lucy, Peter and Andrew close behind him.

"We were trying to figure out if something like a flare would-" Nick began, breaking off with a shout as the phoenix charm between his fingers burnt him. As everyone's eyes fell to the charm it began to glow bright blue.

Pulling Rose's necklace off, Nick cast it to the ground before it could burn him again. Silently the five of them stared at it vaguely aware of the shouts from the battle that was approaching them. For several seconds it seemed to pulse, growing slowly brighter, until, with a blinding flash a stream of light erupted from it, like a bolt of lightning, streaking skywards.

With a thunderous bang cloaked figures appeared by the gates that Andrew had left open. In an instant Nick thought he saw Numquam leading his followers towards them before his vision was obscured as the ghost of a phoenix flew in front of him. For a moment no one moved as it settled on top of one of the gas containers.

In a blaze of spells Nick grabbed hold of Lucy's hand, dragging her towards the concrete bunker that Andrew had shown to them. George and Peter followed, Andrew a little further behind them. Glancing behind him, Nick caught the briefest of glimpses of Numquam turning his attention to the phoenix before he tripped, falling down the steps into the bunker, Lucy crashing down to the ground with him.

Rolling to a stop Nick opened his eyes, for a split second of silence his eyes connected with hers as she landed on top of him. The silence was broken by her scream as a tremendous explosion shook the floor that they were laying on. It told Nick that their plan had worked; a stray spell had hit one of the gas tanks.

As the dust settled in the bunker Nick looked around. On the floor near the door George and Peter were stirring, both of them had been thrown from their feet by the explosion. Helping Lucy to her feet Nick moved towards the door, peering through the smoke that flooded skyward. Somewhere in the distance he saw a dark figure with a limp hurrying away.

Emerging into the rain Nick saw bodies strewn across the ground, the majority of them lying motionless, pools of blood slowly spreading outwards. Behind him he heard a cry of anguish, Peter forcing his way past him moments later. Amongst the bodies that scattered the floor was Andrew, his eyes open, staring vacantly towards the sky.

As Nick watched Peter grieving for his brother he was vaguely aware of more figures emerging from the smoke, all of them dressed in blue robes. The Heart of the Dragon had arrived. Some of them cheered, shouting to all that could hear that Numquam was gone.

Ignoring their voices Nick walked forwards, the phoenix charm that Rose had given him drawing his attention. Stopping before it he bent down, hooking the chain over one finger as he lifted it to examine it.

Even after the explosion it had remained unscratched. Carefully he returned it to its place around his neck.

"He's gone," cried one of the approaching figures. "At last we are free."

"I don't think so," said Nick as Lucy appeared at his side. "He will be back and when he does return he will want revenge."

"You really think he will be back?" whispered Lucy. As he looked at her he could see the fear in her eyes, he could hear it in her voice.

"Yes, I think he will be," Nick replied as he ran his finger over the phoenix. "And I think it will be worse than ever."

"What do we do now?" she asked.

"We regroup, rebuild and prepare for whatever is to come," said Nick. "Numquam will be back and he will come looking for revenge. I think it's far from over."

ACKNOWLEDGEMENTS

I would like to give thanks to the following people for all their support, encouragement and advice during the writing of this book. Without them it wouldn't be where it is today.

To my editor, Thelma Nunn, for her thoughtful adjustments which ended up making the book so much better. And to my mother and father who always found time for the numerous proof-reads and always offered their honest opinions and advice.

To Oskar Gudlagsson, my Icelandic tour guide. Without you the second half of this book would have been impossible. For your knowledge of Icelandic Runes, which I have adapted slightly, and for showing me Asbyrgi canyon which became so influential, you have my eternal thanks.

To Andrew Coghill for his thoughts on 'life's chess game' that have revolutionised the way in which I think and influenced my thoughts on what immortality really is.

And to James Nicholls who helped with the cover design for this book as well as being supportive and understanding through the tough patches in the way only a fellow writer can.

And finally to Liam Warren. For having been there all these years. Without your encouragement and support along the way I may never have got this far.

Lightning Source UK Ltd.
Milton Keynes UK
UKOW050620111111

181873UK00001B/5/P